"You don't need m...

No way did she want to ... with Rick. She was havi... maintaining her emotion... ...um across the room. It was only memories of the blinding pain he'd caused that kept her from being swept away by his charm.

"Don't you want to go with us?" Bobby asked. Oh, she was going to have to find a way to resist this kid.

"Yeah, don't you want to go with us?" Rick mimicked, closing the distance between them. His smile was wicked and way too sexy for her comfort.

She looked away, but not before seeing the mischief dancing in Rick's eyes. She directed her response to his son. "You don't need me."

"Yes, I do," Bobby admitted quietly. His little-boy vulnerability squeezed her heart, dissolving the last of her resistance.

"Okay. I'll come."

* * *

SWEET BRIAR SWEETHEARTS:
There's something about Sweet Briar

Dear Reader,

There is a well-known saying about not judging people until you've walked a mile in their shoes. That saying definitely applies to the heroine of this story, Charlotte Shields.

I have to admit I didn't like Charlotte when I first met her in *How to Steal the Lawman's Heart*. She was Carmen's older and incredibly unfriendly sister. Anyone who has or is a good sister knows that's not the way we treat each other.

I wrote more stories set in Sweet Briar, but I couldn't get Charlotte out of my mind. There had to be more to her than met the eye. She had to be worthy of a happy ending. I just had to see past the proud, prickly outside to the woman she was inside. Of course, the woman inside was just as proud and prickly, but with a soft heart that might be convinced to give love one more chance.

A throwaway sentence in *How to Steal the Lawman's Heart* shaped Charlotte's backstory. She'd been left at the altar by her fiancé. Surely that would be enough to turn a woman's heart to ice. As is often the case, the only man who can melt the ice and help her heal is the one who broke her heart. Enter Dr. Rick Tyler. Now a single father, he returns to Sweet Briar in an attempt to restore his relationship with his young son. And if he can win Charlotte back? Well, all the better.

I hope you enjoy your return to Sweet Briar. I love hearing from my readers, so feel free to visit my website, kathydouglassbooks.com, and drop me a line. While you're there, join my mailing list. I'm also on Facebook. As always, thank you for your support.

Happy reading!

Kathy

Winning Charlotte Back

—

Kathy Douglass

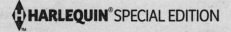

H❖**HARLEQUIN**® SPECIAL EDITION

Recycling programs
for this product may
not exist in your area.

ISBN-13: 978-1-335-57363-6

Winning Charlotte Back

Printed in U.S.A.

Kathy Douglass came by her love of reading naturally—both of her parents were readers. She would finish one book and pick up another. Then she attended law school and traded romances for legal opinions.

After the birth of her two children, her love of reading turned into a love of writing. Kathy now spends her days writing the small-town contemporary novels she enjoys reading.

Books by Kathy Douglass

Harlequin Special Edition

Sweet Briar Sweethearts

How to Steal the Lawman's Heart
The Waitress's Secret
The Rancher and the City Girl
Winning Charlotte Back

This book is dedicated to my husband and sons,
who love and support me in all that I do.
I love you all very much.

This book is also dedicated to Della
for her constant support and encouragement.

Chapter One

As Charlotte Shields passed the secretaries' lunch room on her way to her corner office, the off-key strains of the happy birthday song wafted through the open door. Her steps slowed. Stopped.

"Open my gift first," a voice cried out.

"Wait until after the cake," someone said and female laughter followed.

Charlotte yearned to join the celebration, but she knew she wouldn't be welcome. Not now. Early in her career several of the other women had invited her to join them on a girls' night out. She'd longed to say yes, but she'd known better. The morning of her first day, her father had called her into his office and given her a list of rules designed especially for her. Primary among them was that she was not to mingle with the employees. To his way of thinking, it would be hard to discipline or terminate a friend. She'd been eager to please and convinced that her father knew better than she how to run a business, so she'd complied.

After a while, the invitations slowed and finally stopped. The offers of friendship dried up. The other women came to regard her as conceited and unfriendly, a reputation she'd lived up to over the years. She regretted her behavior now, but years ago she'd been willing to do anything to avoid disappointing her father.

Charlotte's need to please her father had always been her downfall.

She forced the longing and regrets away and continued through the maze of cubicles, pausing when she got to her secretary's desk. "Did anyone call while I was out?"

"Yes, Ms. Shields." Anita handed her a stack of pink paper. "Your father has scheduled a meeting in the conference room for three this afternoon."

"Thank you."

Although Anita was only a year younger than Charlotte's own thirty-four, she never addressed Charlotte by her first name, something that hadn't bothered Charlotte before. For some reason, the distance it created between them bugged her now.

Charlotte opened her mouth to ask how the other woman's pregnancy was progressing, but she couldn't find the words.

"Is there something else, Ms. Shields?" Anita asked when Charlotte continued to stand there. Anita's voice was professional, lacking the warmth that was there when she interacted with the other secretaries, and Charlotte's heart sank.

"No, nothing."

Stepping through the door to her office, Charlotte riffled through the messages. Nothing urgent. Her mind returned to the meeting her father had scheduled for that afternoon. Charles was a creature of habit and had established a schedule that hadn't changed in all the years she'd worked here. The fact that he'd called an impromptu meeting was unsettling. But there was no sense asking him about the agenda beforehand because he wouldn't tell her. Although she was his daughter, he never treated her better than anyone else. If anything, he was harder on her.

She had master's degrees in both business and marketing, but she'd still had to start at the bottom and work her way up to the position of executive vice president of marketing. There was not the slightest doubt in her mind that had she been a son, her path would have been easier. By now, she'd be president.

She got down to work, determined to have her desk cleared in case her father passed out new assignments.

At promptly 2:55 she stepped into the conference room. Several executives mingled, talking quietly among themselves. They nodded at her and she did the same. She was too jittery to engage in conversation, so she stared at the framed newspaper and magazine articles lining the walls. The articles chronicled the progression of Shields Manufacturing from a small company specializing in bookcases to one of the top furniture manufacturing companies in the world.

Five minutes later her father entered, followed by a man she'd never seen before.

"Have a seat," Charles said. The man he'd brought with him took the chair at her father's right—her chair—so she was forced to sit in the next chair. She glowered at the trespasser but he didn't seem to notice.

Instead of immediately getting to the point of the meeting as was his habit, Charles's eyes traveled the same path hers had only moments ago, a small smile on his face as he seemed to relive the history of the company. For the briefest moment, her father seemed reflective. Charles was many things, but introspective wasn't one of them.

Was he ill? He'd lost weight since her mother's death two years ago, but she'd attributed it to lack of appetite due to grief. She looked at him closely. She didn't notice anything different.

"I know you're all wondering why I called this meeting today." Charles smiled. Smiled! He never smiled. Charlotte's heart sped up as worry gnawed at her.

"Let me put you at ease," Charles continued. "I'm not sick. And you all know the company is doing well."

Relief whooshed through Charlotte. Although Charles wasn't the warmest person, he was for all intents and purposes the only family she had, as she was currently estranged from her sisters.

She realized her father was still speaking and forced herself to listen. Charles gestured to the wall. "We've come a long way from where we started to where we are now. I want to ensure that the next thirty-five years are just as successful as the past thirty-five. To that end, I'm stepping aside as president to make room for someone new. I'll stay on as CEO to make sure the company continues to go in the right direction."

Everyone in the room began to talk, but Charlotte couldn't find her voice. Her heart drummed in anticipation. Her father was finally going to reward her with the job she'd worked and sacrificed for. All her hard work, her long days and lonely nights were finally going to pay off.

Charles cleared his throat and the room grew silent. He smiled at the man beside him and unease began to churn in Charlotte's stomach. "This is Gabriel Jenkins. As of noon today, he's the new president."

Her father continued to talk, but Charlotte couldn't make out any of the words over the buzzing in her head. He couldn't do this to her. She'd dedicated her life to him. To this company. And he was bringing in a stranger to run it! Someone who hadn't shed one tear or sweated one ounce of blood to make Shields Manufacturing the success that it was. He'd betrayed her. And he expected her to join in the applause and well wishes?

She fought against the dizziness and the black hole that threatened to swallow her. She ignored the pain that resulted from her heart being ripped out of her chest and focused her attention on her father. He wasn't even looking at her, but rather was paying rapt attention to the interloper who was now rambling about his Harvard education.

She looked around the room at the rest of the executives. Most seemed embarrassed or hurt for her and looked away. Only Toby Baker met her eyes, and he was smirking. He'd asked her out a couple of times, but even with her limited experience with men, she'd known he was only looking to get ahead by dating the boss's daughter. Get ahead. That was a laugh.

She'd sacrificed everything for her father and this stupid company. And what had that blind loyalty gotten her? No friends. No family of her own. No relationship with her sisters. Nothing.

Anger burned her stomach and grew into a raging inferno. She stood, pushing her chair so hard that, despite the thick carpet, it slammed against the wall. Every eye turned in her direction and the new president stopped babbling. Her father raised an imperial eyebrow that in the past would have had her cowering and slinking back into her seat. Not this time. She'd lost everything that mattered. There was nothing more for her to lose.

"Charlotte." Her father's tone was severe. Cold. No different from the look in his eyes or the ice encasing his heart.

"I quit." She glanced at her watch. "Effective three thirteen p.m."

Her father didn't blink or acknowledge her words in the slightest. Milton Hayes, an old-timer and the closest thing she had to a friend in the company, nodded once as if agreeing with her move. The new president looked startled and opened his mouth as if to speak, but she no longer had to listen to anyone. Brushing past him, she walked to her office. She had very few personal items there, only a throw on the back of her chair that she used on damp or chilly days to keep her feet warm and an old snapshot of her with her mother and sisters. She dropped the picture into her purse, grabbed the throw and turned off the light.

"Mr. Adams from the First Bank of America is holding on line four," Anita said when Charlotte approached.

"He is no longer my problem," Charlotte said, not slowing as she passed the woman who could have been a friend if Charlotte had taken her up on one of her many overtures. Another foolish move she'd made in the futile effort to gain her father's approval. Charlotte stalked to the elevator then pressed the button several times, anxious to get out of this place.

Finally the elevator door slid open. Blinking back hot tears, she stepped inside. She refused to let even one teardrop fall. She squeezed her eyes shut and breathed deeply until she'd smothered the urge to cry. Crying didn't change anything; it only gave someone else power over you.

After dumping her belongings onto the passenger seat of her car, she sped out of the garage. Shields Manufacturing was in her past and she wasn't looking back.

By the time she was sitting on the sofa in her duplex, the anger and numbness had worn off and the magnitude of what she'd done hit her, making her sick to her stomach.

She'd quit her job.

She wasn't worried about money. She'd invested wisely and lived well within her means. But she'd severed the link to the only family member she had a relationship with. The relationship she'd done everything to hang on to. And it had cost her everything. She'd all but given up her life to earn her father's love and now knew it had been for nothing. He didn't care a thing about her and nothing she did would ever change that.

She forced the nausea away. She'd survived worse things and come out a wiser, stronger person. She'd survive this, too.

"Almost there," Rick Tyler said, infusing his voice with enthusiasm. He stole a look at his brooding ten-year-old stepson then focused back on the road, steering the U-Haul around a curve.

"Big whoop."

Rick bit back a sigh. To say Bobby had resisted moving from Milwaukee would be an understatement. But then, he'd expected resistance. Bobby had fought Rick tooth and nail about everything since his mother walked out on them a year and a half ago. They hadn't heard a word from her since and they didn't have a way of contacting her.

"Sweet Briar is a great place. Even though I grew up in New Jersey, I spent a lot of time here when I was in college. I actually worked at a furniture manufacturing company for a couple of summers."

"You know how to make furniture?" Bobby asked, his eyes sparking with a hint of interest.

"No. Actually, I worked in the main office."

The gleam left Bobby's eyes. Rick couldn't blame him. Shuffling papers didn't hold nearly the excitement of using big tools. And his experiences had convinced him that corporate America wasn't for him. Though Rick had hated the work, he'd enjoyed his time with the boss's daughter.

Charlotte had been sweet and funny, if a little too eager to please her father, something he'd suffered from as well. They'd gotten close and their fathers had pressured them to get engaged.

Rick knew he shouldn't have gone along with the plan as long as he had, but things had spun out of control so quickly. It had gone from simple talk to a fait accompli in a matter of weeks. And he had loved Charlotte, even though he hadn't been *in love* with her.

As the wedding date drew closer, Rick's doubts had increased. Their parents were calling all the shots and he had felt trapped.

His father had wanted Rick to join the family business. After all, he would soon have a wife to support. Rick's dream of going to medical school had been going up in flames in front of his eyes. He'd needed to stop things. He'd tried and tried to get Charlotte to call off the wedding.

When she wouldn't agree, he hadn't shown up at the church.

He'd hated hurting her, but he'd been desperate. He'd cared enough about her not to marry her when he'd known he'd only grow to resent her if he couldn't follow his dreams. In the long run, it had been best for both of them. At least that was what he told himself when the guilt kept him awake at night.

"If it was so great then why didn't you stay?"

"I'd been accepted to University of Michigan medical school." His life had moved forward and the town had become a part of his past. But he hadn't forgotten the time he'd spent with Charlotte. The summer they'd spent in the quaint town had been one of the best of his life. Sweet Briar seemed like the perfect place to start over and raise a family.

Of course, even as he believed it would be good for Bobby, he knew he had some bridges to repair, starting with Charlotte. He'd tried to apologize to her for leaving her at the altar, but he hadn't succeeded. If he was going to move here, he was going to have to make amends to her. Additionally, he had to prove to the people of the town that he was worthy of being their doctor.

Jake Patterson, his mentor from medical school, had relatives in the area. He'd been the one to mention the town's needs. The longtime doctor had died three years ago, leaving the people of Sweet Briar to travel to Willow Creek for medical care. Two other doctors had come and gone after him. When Dr. Patterson put Rick's name forward, he reported back that several members of the town council and a few older residents in town expressed reservations about Rick. They remembered him as the runaway groom who'd thoughtlessly left one of their own standing at the church. They weren't sure they could count on him to live up to a commitment.

Even though Rick didn't need anyone's approval to open a practice, he'd reached out to the mayor and the council. Rick had promised the mayor that he'd stay at least two years. Still, he knew he had a lot of hard work to do if he intended to show the people of Sweet Briar that he was reliable.

Of course, winning over the town was only part of his problem. He also needed to find a way to make amends to Charlotte. That was a key factor in deciding to return to Sweet Briar. He didn't like the way he'd ended things between them. After what happened with Sherry, it became imperative to him that he make things right with Charlotte. He needed to do it in person.

Twelve years ago he'd known he'd hurt her, but hadn't realized just how much. Then his ex-wife left him and he'd gotten a taste of the pain Charlotte must have experienced. The humiliation. Now Rick knew he'd blown a hole in Charlotte's heart when he didn't show up at the church. No matter how desperate he'd felt, he should have shown up. He didn't imagine seeing her again would be pleasant, but he didn't deserve it to be. What he'd done had been reprehensible. He knew that now. He only wished he'd known it then. He'd telephoned her the day after to apologize, but she hadn't accepted his call. He'd written two letters, but they'd been returned unopened. He hadn't contacted her again.

He and Bobby rode in silence for a while. When Bobby spoke his voice was tiny. Scared. "Mom won't know how to find me. She'll come back and someone else will be living in our house."

Rick doubted she'd ever return. Sherry was too busy enjoying the single life. Not that he would ever say that to his son. "I left our information with the Browns next door. If she stops by they'll tell her where we are. And I have the same cell phone number. If your mom tries to reach us, she'll be able to. Okay?"

"Sure, Rick." Sarcasm barely disguised the worry in his voice.

Rick sighed and counted to ten. The counselor Rick had taken Bobby to see had insisted his son was testing him because he was afraid Rick would abandon him, too. Rick had known that without being told. What he didn't know was how to help Bobby.

"You've called me Dad for years. I'd appreciate it if you didn't call me Rick now."

"Or what? You'll write a stupid letter and sneak out in the middle of the night, leaving me all alone?" Bobby's voice quivered and tears flooded his eyes.

Rick clapped a hand on his son's shoulder. "That's not going to happen. You're my son and I love you. Where I go, you go. Got it?"

Blinking furiously, Bobby nodded and turned to stare out his window. Rick once more cursed his ex-wife. Okay, so she didn't want to be married to him anymore—he got that. But he couldn't believe she no longer wanted her son. How was Rick supposed to help Bobby deal with that kind of rejection?

Hopefully Sweet Briar would provide the answers Rick was searching for. Bobby had gone from being sad, refusing to leave home in case his mother returned, to angry. He'd also begun hanging around the wrong kids and getting into trouble. He'd stopped doing his homework and become disruptive in class. His teacher had been sympathetic, but she'd had other students to consider. When the principal suggested enrolling Bobby in an alternative school, Rick had known he needed to act.

Rick didn't delude himself into believing that Bobby's problems would magically disappear in Sweet Briar. But Rick would be running a small practice here, so he'd have more time to spend with his son than he'd had in Milwaukee. That had to help. If not, Rick didn't know what he would do. He just knew he wouldn't stop until he found the solution.

He slowed, checking the numbers on the houses, searching for the address the rental agent had given him. Rick had been lucky to find the duplex. Sweet Briar didn't have much of a rental market and the other two available options weren't as nice as the three-bedroom unit with a backyard that the agent had found. The agent said the place wouldn't be on the market for long, so Rick had taken the property sight unseen, renting it for a year.

He spotted the address and slowed, parking the truck on the street. "We're here. Home at last."

Bobby hopped out of the truck, reached behind the seat and grabbed his basketball, then began dribbling it on the driveway.

"Let's get everything unloaded before you play. I want to get the beds set up. Then we can grab something to eat."

Bobby huffed out a breath but he dropped the ball on the grass and walked toward the back of the truck. His movements were turtle-slow but at least he was cooperating.

Rick took care of releasing his Mustang from the tow and pulled into his half of the shared driveway, next to a midnight blue BMW sedan. Then he unlocked the truck and raised the door.

"Looks like our neighbor is home," Rick said as he moved a couple of boxes, trying to find one that wasn't too heavy for Bobby. He'd packed carefully, so the load hadn't shifted too much during the drive.

Bobby took the box and grunted as he pressed it against his chest. He frowned. "That's an old person's car. It's probably some grumpy old man who's going to yell at me to keep off his grass."

"Look at those flowers. They don't look like something a grumpy old man would plant. Maybe a nice old lady who likes to bake cookies lives there."

"And she'll yell at me to keep out of her garden."

Rick didn't get a chance to reply because the front door opened and a woman stepped outside. He only got a brief glance at her before she turned away from him, but it was enough to reveal that she wasn't an old lady. He guessed she was about thirty. She wasn't much taller than average, but what she lacked in height she made up for in curves. No doubt she was married or involved. Not that it mattered. Bobby had to be his main concern. He didn't have room in his life for a relationship. Still, since they were going to be sharing a wall, it wouldn't hurt to be friendly.

"Come on, Bobby. Let's introduce ourselves."

Bobby rolled his eyes but he followed Rick across the yard to the short flight of stairs, juggling the box as he went. As they grew closer, the woman turned around. Rick got a good look at her face and his heart skipped a beat.

Charlotte.

Chapter Two

This could not be happening.

Charlotte stared at the man who'd left her dressed in her wedding gown and standing alone in front of a church filled with everyone she knew twelve years ago. He had to be a figment of her imagination. A trick her mind was playing on her after the horrible day she'd had. She blinked as if she could make him vanish. No such luck. Rick still stood there, a stunned expression on his face. In that moment she once again felt the embarrassment and horror as what was supposed to be the happiest day of her life had turned into a living nightmare when she realized her fiancé really wasn't going to show. Her heart sped up and her knees nearly buckled. Pride had her stiffening her spine and lifting her chin. She hadn't fallen apart then and she wouldn't fall apart now.

"Rick." She infused the word with all the displeasure she felt.

He smiled cautiously as if not sure how she would react to seeing him. Could he really be in doubt? "Charlotte."

She only glared at him, hoping he'd see the anger in her expression and leave.

"Wow. You look great." He put his foot on the bottom step as if to close the distance between them. She moved back until she bumped into her door. Was he serious? They weren't old friends about to embrace and catch up on the past. He'd left her at the altar. Didn't he know that callous act had wiped out their previous friendship, making them enemies for life? Heck, their descendants would be enemies for generations to come.

"Dad. I thought we were going to unpack and get something to eat. I'm hungry."

Her eyes immediately shifted to the boy who was staring at her, a frown marring his face. The kid looked to be about ten or eleven. Pain pierced her chest. Rick couldn't have waited long after dumping her before he'd met someone else and started a family. Charlotte wondered if Rick's father had chosen that girl as well or if Rick had done his own choosing. He'd sworn he hadn't been ready to marry. He said he had plans and dreams and marriage didn't fit into them. Apparently he just hadn't wanted to marry her.

"Bobby, say hello."

The kid muttered the most unfriendly greeting she'd received in years. Given the fact that she was universally disliked, that was saying something.

"Hi yourself." Her tone wasn't any friendlier and the kid gave her an odd look. His eyes widened in surprise and the corners of his mouth twitched. For a moment she thought he might smile. Instead, he tightened his grip on the box and trekked across her grass, smashing a couple of flowers in the process. She didn't even wince. She felt like smashing a couple herself.

"We're moving in next door," Rick said unnecessarily.

She'd figured that out on her own. "Why?"

"We're looking for a fresh start."

"And of all the places in the world, you chose my town?"

He shuffled his feet. "I always liked it here. The people are warm and welcoming, which is what Bobby needs right now."

"The same could be said of many small towns across America."

"Maybe, but we'd be strangers somewhere else. I have friends here."

"I hope you don't count me among them."

He had the good grace to look embarrassed. "I'd like to apologize again."

"Again?" Her voice rose and she struggled to control it. "I must have missed the first time. Surely you don't think sending a note by your best man saying 'Charlotte, I'm sorry you don't agree we shouldn't get married' qualifies as an apology for not showing up at the church."

He hung his head for a minute before straightening. To his credit he met her eyes. She saw shame there. Good. He should be ashamed. "You're right. It doesn't. I'm sorry, Charlotte. But I couldn't get you to agree that we shouldn't get married just to please our fathers. I felt the walls closing in and I panicked. That's not an excuse and it doesn't make me look good, but it's the truth. I know I hurt and embarrassed you. You didn't deserve that. Please forgive me."

"Not in this lifetime."

"Charlotte," he began, but she cut him off. Whatever he had to say would be too little too late.

"But don't worry, Rick. I won't tell your wife what a jerk you are. If she hasn't discovered it yet, I'm sure she will soon."

"I no longer have a wife. I'm divorced."

"I guess she figured it out on her own. Clearly she's smarter than I was. Good for her."

His lips compressed, but he didn't reply. Instead, he turned on his heel and followed his son across the grass and into the house.

Charlotte watched him leave, telling herself her blood was pounding through her veins because she'd been shocked to see Rick again, and not because she had any residual feelings for him.

As if pulled by a force stronger than her will, she went inside her house and headed toward the third and mostly unused bedroom. She always kept the door closed as if that would hold the memories at bay. Most days it worked. But not today. Not after seeing Rick. The memories were swirling around her head, poking her battered heart from every direction.

Turning the knob, she walked to the closet and opened the door. There, hanging in heavy plastic, was her wedding dress. Covered in lace and beads, it had been the most beautiful gown in the entire store. She'd known when she'd laid eyes upon it that she would feel like a princess wearing it. And she had. Until the minute when she'd been forced to face the fact that her groom wasn't coming.

He'd talked for days about calling off the whole thing, becoming more persistent as time passed, but she'd thought he'd just had cold feet. He'd wanted her to go with him to tell their parents they didn't want to get married, but she'd refused. Sure, their fathers had engineered the whole thing, enamored of the idea of joining their families as well as their businesses, but she hadn't minded. She'd fallen in love with Rick and thought he'd felt the same. He'd seemed to enjoy being with her and they'd come close to making love on more than one occasion. She'd been sure that had meant something. She'd believed when he had time to think about their future together and how happy she'd make him, he'd come to his senses and they'd get married as planned and live happily ever after.

She'd been wrong.

She brushed her hands over the plastic bag protecting her dress from the elements then closed the door on the reminder of what happened when she followed her heart instead of her head. She wouldn't make that mistake again.

Rick rang Charlotte's doorbell then inhaled deeply as he waited for her to come to the door. He knew she was home because her car was still parked in the driveway and the sounds of Motown filtered through her open front window. He couldn't believe they were neighbors. He'd been planning to look her up in a day or two and apologize to her, but this was better, if unexpected. He'd seen the pain in her eyes that she'd tried to cover. Guilt had clogged his throat, making it difficult to breathe.

He could tell his presence hurt her, something he didn't want to do. After seeing her reaction, he'd contacted his rental agent about getting out of his lease, but it was ironclad. Even if he could get out of it, he'd have to find another place to live, disrupting Bobby yet again. Somehow he had to heal the wound he'd inflicted so Charlotte wouldn't be uncomfortable with him living next door.

He'd tried to apologize earlier, but even to him the words had fallen short. How did he express how sorry he was for leaving her alone on what should have been their wedding day? He'd known at the time that the note he'd scribbled at the last minute had been insufficient, so he'd called her the next morning, but she wouldn't speak to him.

When the two letters he'd written to her had been returned unopened, he should have taken that as a sign of just how hurt she'd been and kept trying to reach her but he didn't. He convinced himself that she didn't want to hear from him and that he should honor her wish. That was a poor excuse and he'd known it at the time. His only explanation was that he'd been young and dumb and looking for an easy way out of a difficult situation. Twelve years later he was older and hopefully wiser. He wouldn't walk away after one effort to beg her forgiveness. So he hadn't let more than the hour it had taken to unload the truck and talk to his Realtor pass before he made a second effort.

The door swung open. "What are you doing here?"

"I hoped we could talk."

"I hoped to never see you again, yet here you are."

"Charlotte, we were friends once. I know I ruined that friendship and that you don't owe me anything. But can we talk for a few minutes? Please?"

She was quiet so long he wondered if she had any intention of replying. "Five minutes. I'm only agreeing to this so you'll leave me alone. Got it?"

He backed up, letting her step outside. Although she had two chairs on her front porch, she leaned against the wall and folded her arms over her chest. Despite the serious conversation he wanted to have, he couldn't help noticing how sexy she was. How good she smelled.

He steered his mind back where it belonged. Five minutes wasn't long, so he cut to the chase. "I shouldn't have left you alone at the church, Charlotte. I should have been there beside you."

"So why'd you do it?" Her voice was so soft it barely carried to him, but the pain and confusion came through loud and clear. Regret made his heart ache.

"Honestly? I was scared that I'd give in to the pressure. I wanted my father's approval in the worst way. The same way you wanted your father's. But I came to realize getting married and sacrificing our dreams in order to fulfill theirs was too high a price to pay." He heaved a sigh as he remembered the pressure he'd been under at the time. Even at twenty-two he'd known a marriage under those circumstances was doomed. He just hadn't known soon enough. "We would have been miserable. I thought if we presented a united front and told them we didn't want to get married they'd have to agree we were making a mistake. But I couldn't convince you to stand with me."

"So you're saying it's my fault you didn't show."

"No. Not at all. The fault was all mine. I took the coward's way out and you were left all alone to face everyone. No one could ever fault you for what I did."

Charlotte blew out a breath. "My father accused me of doing something to drive you away."

"What? That's insane. You didn't do anything wrong. We shouldn't have been forced to marry just to suit them. They didn't need us to be married in order to merge their businesses."

"And yet the merger didn't happen."

"Not our fault."

She shrugged. "Are we done?"

"Do you accept my apology?"

"What difference could it possibly make now?"

He looked into her beautiful eyes, hoping he could see some emotion there. He didn't. If she felt anything, she wasn't willing to share it with him. "Haven't you ever done something you regretted? Hurt someone you cared about? Wouldn't you want their forgiveness, no matter how late your apology was in coming?"

She closed her eyes. "Fine. I forgive you. Now if there's nothing else…"

He wished he believed her, but he knew she was saying whatever it took to get rid of him. Gaining her forgiveness would take time.

"Just one more thing. I want you to know that I contacted my Realtor and tried to get out of my lease. I can't. So as much as I hate to do it to you, we're stuck as neighbors."

She blew out an exasperated breath. "That it? Or do you have some other bad news to drop on me?"

"No. That's it." He'd pressed her as far as he dared. He needed to give her space. Besides, he needed to get back to Bobby. "Good night."

She didn't answer, but then, he didn't expect her to. After the way he'd hurt her, he didn't deserve forgiveness that easily. But it was a start. At this point, he would take it.

"How long is this going to take?" Bobby asked as Rick parked in front of the medical building the next morning. Bobby had been grumbling since Rick told him he couldn't stay home alone. The town was small and safe, but Rick wasn't comfortable leaving his son on his own for more than a few minutes. Once he and Bobby got settled, he was going to find someone to watch Bobby until school started.

"Not long. I told you I want to get a look around and see what I need to do." Agreeing to set up the practice sight unseen had been risky, but Rick saw this as both a professional and personal opportunity. He'd relied on information provided by the mayor in conversations over the past several months and photos provided by the real-estate agent. This was the first time he would see his building in person. Hopefully those pictures were accurate.

"What am I supposed to do?"

"I told you to plan on occupying yourself. You could have brought a book. If you don't plan—"

"Yeah, I know. I'll get waylaid and end up where I don't want to be. Like here."

"Bobby."

"Never mind. I'll just sit in the car and listen to the radio."

"Not a chance." Rick removed the key from the ignition and stepped out. After fixing Rick with a glare and heaving a sigh so heavy he must have pulled oxygen from his toes, Bobby got out of the car and slammed the door just in case Rick hadn't picked up on his annoyance.

A man of about Rick's height was walking in their direction. He smiled. "Are you Dr. Tyler?"

"Yes."

The man offered his hand. "I'm Lex Devlin."

"Mr. Mayor. It's nice to meet you."

"Call me Lex." He turned his attention to Bobby. "Hi. You must be Bobby."

To his credit, despite how annoyed he was with Rick, his son was polite. "Yes. It's nice to meet you, sir."

Lex nodded. "I'm here to answer any questions you might have."

"Thanks. We were just about to have a look around. You're welcome to join us."

The inside of the building was as tidily kept as the outside. Although it hadn't been used in some time, there wasn't the grime he expected. He ran a finger across the counter separating the empty waiting area from the examination rooms. Not a speck of dust.

"Sweet Briar is a great place to live, but lately we've had a hard time keeping a doctor. Our last doctor got married and moved to Boston after six months because his wife wanted to live near her family. The one before only lasted three months before deciding that although she wanted to live in a small town, she didn't mean one this small. Everyone was so excited about having a doctor make a two-year commitment that several people got together and cleaned the offices last week."

"Wow. Thanks."

"Don't thank me. I didn't do anything. But I will pass your appreciation along to those who actually did the work."

Rick walked past the counter. There was enough space for two workstations as well as file cabinets. He continued down the hall and opened the first of six doors. The room was large and the sun streamed through the big window on the far wall. He could envision two examination tables as well as a desk, scale, guest chair and other equipment fitting in the space. Three other rooms were the same size, and there were two smaller ones that could be used as offices.

A second hallway led to a bathroom and a room that could be used as a break room. Although the walls could use a fresh coat of paint, he was pleased by what he saw.

"When do you think you'll be ready to start seeing patients?"

"I hope within the next three weeks. I need to hire a nurse and a receptionist, but I can muddle along without them at first if need be. The truck bringing my office furniture should arrive in a few days."

"I'll put out the word about the employees you need. It shouldn't be hard for you to find someone qualified around here."

"Thanks. I appreciate that."

Rick let the mayor out then walked through the offices once more. Excitement swept through him along with the desire to share the experience with someone. His ex-wife was long gone. Not that he and Sherry had shared much toward the end of their marriage. Bobby was here, but he was too angry to share Rick's happiness. Charlotte had been his closest friend in Sweet Briar, and once upon a time she would have been beside him, sharing his joy. They weren't friends now. He'd ruined that years ago with his selfish behavior.

He blew out a breath, his excitement diminished by regret.

"Can we leave now?" Bobby asked. "All you're doing is staring into space. You can do that at home."

Rick threw his arm over his son's shoulder. There was no sense looking back at a past he couldn't change. He needed to concentrate on the present. "Yes. We can leave."

Rick locked the door, glad for the moment that Bobby hadn't shrugged off his arm. Things were looking up.

Chapter Three

Charlotte's stomach growled as she closed the cabinet door on her newly organized dishes. Over the past couple of days she'd cleaned her house from top to bottom, removing every speck of dust from every crack and crevice. She swiped a hand over her forehead, wiping away perspiration. Maybe she would paint. One of her secret pleasures was watching home renovations shows. She didn't kid herself that she had what it took to gut her kitchen and rebuild it, but surely she could put in a new tile backsplash. And maybe while she was changing her house, she could find a way to change her life.

After her stomach rumbled again, she decided it was time to quit for the day and get something to eat. Her appetite had waned over the past few days and she'd skipped meals. She knew part of the reason for her loss of appetite was the death of her lifelong dream of one day running Shields Manufacturing. The job represented more than professional achievement. It would have been proof that her father really did love her and that everything she'd sacrificed to gain that love had been worth it. Watching him give that job to someone else smashed that delusion. Her father didn't love her. She'd only been kidding herself.

He hadn't called her to explain his actions, or to ask her to return. He hadn't even had his secretary call to see if she was all right. It was as if she no longer existed. She shouldn't be surprised. He'd turned his back on her sister Carmen just as easily. Carmen had been a bit of a wild child as a teenager, bringing shame on the family. When she was eighteen, she'd been involved in a fatal car accident. Carmen hadn't been driving, nor had she been drinking, but that hadn't mattered to their father. He'd thrown her out of the house and washed his hands of her. To her shame, Charlotte had joined her father in order to gain his approval, rejecting the little sister who'd loved her. When Carmen returned to town a couple of years ago, she'd reached out. Charlotte had repeatedly rejected her. What a fool she'd been.

Of course, her job situation was only part of the reason she'd skipped meals and was having trouble sleeping. The biggest part was residing on the other side of her shared wall. She'd managed to avoid Rick for the past three days, but she'd been aware of his presence. She'd seen him coming and going, but he hadn't sought her out again. And that was fine with her. She didn't want to have anything to do with him. Sure, he'd apologized, but so what? It was only words. Empty words that didn't change a thing.

Deciding she'd spent more time than she cared to thinking about Rick Tyler, she pulled open her refrigerator door. Nothing appealed to her. She wasn't the best cook, and apart from a few simple meals that she made on a regular rotation, she was pretty useless in the kitchen. After the past few rotten days she'd endured, she deserved something good and greasy.

She looked at her clothes. Upholding the family status as leaders in the community had been drilled into her since birth. Appearance had meant everything, so she'd never dreamed of being seen in public wearing jeans and a T-shirt. She might not still work for her father, but some things were too deeply ingrained in her to simply vanish.

Dashing up the stairs, she washed up and changed into a lavender sleeveless blouse and dark purple cropped pants. She pulled a comb through her hair then slid a band over it, to hold it off her face. She added lipstick then pronounced herself ready for the world.

The drive to Mabel's Diner was short and she found a parking space right away. The sun was beginning to set and a cool breeze blew, filling the air with the scent of the flowers overflowing the planters lining the street. Even in the worst of economic times, Sweet Briar had managed to maintain the landscaping. Despite the gloom in her heart, her spirits lifted a little at the sight of the colorful flowers.

Grabbing her book from the passenger seat, Charlotte headed for the diner. She smiled at several people as she passed them but they didn't smile back. She swallowed the pain of their rejection. She'd rejected them first. She'd treated the citizens of Sweet Briar—some of whom worked for her at Shields Manufacturing—like dirt beneath her feet. She'd been scornful, arrogant and downright rude. She deserved to be ignored. She'd earned it.

Besides, they had no way of knowing the kind of

week she'd had and how desperately she needed a smile. Or maybe they did. News traveled faster than light in Sweet Briar. By now everyone could know that her father had given the job she'd lived for to a stranger and that the man who'd ditched her at the altar was back in town. She froze and reconsidered going into the diner. No. She wasn't going to hide like a criminal.

She picked up the pace and walked through the door.

And straight into Rick Tyler and his son.

Great. Sweet Briar was a small town, and she knew they would run into each other from time to time, but now?

"Hi, Charlotte," Rick said cautiously.

"Hi." She didn't return his smile. Maybe if she didn't do anything to encourage conversation, he would take the hint and leave her alone.

"Bobby, say hello."

Or not.

"Hi," the kid said dutifully. There was a sadness in his eyes that she recognized. She saw it in the mirror every morning.

"Hi, Bobby." She smiled at him. After all, she didn't have anything against him.

She looked around, hoping to find an empty booth. After a few minutes, a group of four rose and a busboy began to clear the table. The hostess came up to Rick. "Your table is ready."

Rick turned back to Charlotte. "Are you meeting someone or would you like to join us?"

He smiled again, and despite the fact that he was the last man in the world she wanted to spend time with, her heart skipped a beat and was off to the races. Reminding herself that he'd hurt and humiliated her didn't help. At a couple of inches over six feet with a muscular body, he had always appealed to her. His face had matured over the past dozen years, but he still had those dimples that had always made her go weak in the knees. And darn if her knees didn't feel a little wobbly now.

"I'd rather eat alone."

Rick turned back to the hostess. "How long is the wait?"

"Twenty-five minutes. You're lucky that party finished when they did."

"I don't mind waiting," Charlotte said. "I'm not that hungry." Her stomach chose that moment to growl loudly, giving lie to her words.

Rick's smile wavered, then faded. "I know I hurt you, Charlotte. And I also know my apology didn't take away the pain of seeing me. Sorry for bothering you."

He turned to go but his words echoed in her mind. *Didn't take away the pain?* Did he think she wasn't over being left at the altar after twelve long years? That her poor little heart was still hurting? That she couldn't handle being around him without wanting to dissolve into tears? What kind of weakling did he think she was? No way was she going to live next door to him while he gave her pitying looks. She would show him that Charlotte Shields was stronger than anyone he'd ever met.

"On second thought," she said loud enough to have him pausing midstep, "I am hungry and would prefer not to wait."

He turned back and smiled. "Come on."

They scooted around crowded tables, following the hostess to the vacant booth. She placed the menus on the table then smiled at them. "Your server will be with you soon. Enjoy your meal."

Bobby slid into one side of the booth, and Rick stood aside waiting for Charlotte to sit on the other.

She squelched a sigh when he sat down beside her. The bench was small, but she moved as far away from Rick as she could. She was eating with him to prove a point, but did that require sitting close enough to inhale his cologne?

The waitress appeared, pad in hand, ready to take their orders.

"Could we have another minute?" Rick asked.

"No problem."

"It's nice running into you here," Rick said. "Right, Bobby?"

"Sure," the kid said from behind his menu.

Rick removed the menu from his son's hands and set it on the table. "Bobby, don't be rude."

Charlotte stared at Rick's son. "I brought a book because I was planning to enjoy my meal alone. Your dad is the one who insisted I join you, not the other way around, kid."

Bobby looked like he wasn't sure what to make of her. "He dragged me here, too. I wanted McDonald's."

"Fat chance of that. There isn't a McDonald's for miles around. But Mabel's food is great. I'm getting a double burger and a mega basket of fries. Maybe even some onion rings. And before you ask, I'm not sharing, so if you want some get your own."

The kid's eyes were the size of saucers. "You mean you aren't getting a salad?"

"I hate vegetables. Especially salad. I gave them up for Lent one year and decided to make it a lifestyle. I'm going to use a bunch of ketchup on my fries and you can pretend it's tomatoes if that makes you feel better."

The kid looked at her with something akin to admiration. Hopefully it was a passing phase. She didn't want Bobby to get the idea that they were going to be friends. "I want what you're getting."

She glanced at Rick, who was staring at her like she had two heads. Tough. She wasn't responsible for the kid's diet. If he wanted the boy to eat vegetables he was going to have to fight that battle on his own.

"You're kidding, right?" Rick asked, hope in his eyes. He really did expect her to help him manage his son's diet. Poor thing. He may have asked for her forgiveness and may even regret his actions, but that only got him so far. She'd lived with the pain of his rejection for years. She'd heard the whispers behind her back. Then she'd learned to turn off her heart and keep people at a distance. An apology, no matter how sincerely made, wouldn't turn back time.

"No. The only green thing I eat is pistachio ice cream. And only if they're out of cookies and cream." She looked at the boy again. "Two treats in one. Cookies and ice cream."

Clearly awed, Bobby nodded as if she'd just shared some great wisdom with him.

Rick sputtered and Charlotte nearly laughed out loud. Incredibly, she was having fun. There was something freeing about not worrying about living up to her father's impossible standards.

The waitress came and Charlotte gave her order. Bobby asked for the same thing.

"Make that three with two side salads," Rick said, looking at Bobby.

"I hope they're both for you because I'm giving up vegetables, too." The kid looked at Charlotte. "When is Lent?"

"You're out of luck. It started six weeks before Easter. You missed it."

"Not to mention that we're not Catholic," Rick added.

"Neither am I," Charlotte said.

"You're not helping."

She simply smiled.

The waitress arrived with their orders. They were silent while they added mustard and ketchup to their burgers and fries. Charlotte picked up her burger and took a huge bite. Delicious. She'd pay tomorrow when she had to ride a few more miles on her bike, but for tonight she was going to indulge.

"The town has sure changed since I was here last," Rick said.

"Did you really think everything would be the same after twelve years? Like we were frozen in time or something?" Her answer came out sharper than she intended, but really.

"No. I just mean that it's grown. The downtown is bigger and there are more businesses. When we were driving in I noticed a lot more houses. There have got to be more than the nineteen hundred people the population sign says."

She shrugged, something she had never done in the past. It wasn't decorum. Swirling a fry in her puddle of ketchup, she answered, "There may be a couple hundred more residents. There's a new subdivision on the other side of the lake. I'm not exactly sure if they're in Sweet Briar proper or not. A lot of the people you see in town are tourists."

"Oh."

"What brought you back to town?"

"A job. I'm opening a medical practice."

She felt her eyebrows rise. "You're a doctor? I thought you went back to New Jersey to take over your father's company."

"I never wanted that. I've always wanted to be a doctor. My father wouldn't listen to what I said, so I had to show him with my actions."

"I'm glad it worked out for you."

He winced. Clearly he hadn't missed the sarcasm in her voice. "Charlotte. I know I said it before and I'll keep saying it until you believe me. I am sorry."

"I do believe you, so you can stop apologizing. It just doesn't make a difference. Maybe if you'd apologized as sincerely and in person twelve years ago. Now... I don't care. Okay?"

"I'm ready for dessert," Bobby interrupted, undoubtedly stopping Rick from offering another apology she didn't care to hear.

"Eat your salad first."

Bobby looked at Charlotte as if appealing to her for help. She wiped her mouth and hands, tossed her napkin on the table, then opened her purse and pulled out some cash. "Sorry, kid. You're on your own. I've got to get going."

Rick placed his hand on hers. "Dinner's on me."

"That's not necessary," Charlotte said, pulling her hand away.

"As you pointed out, I invited you to join us and we enjoyed the pleasure of your company. I'm trying to raise my son to know that under those circumstances I should pay the bill. Please."

Far be it from her to stand in the way of Rick raising a proper young man. "Okay. Thanks." She stood and he did the same, letting her pass. "See you around, Bobby."

The kid smiled. "'Bye, Charlotte."

Charlotte walked out of the restaurant without looking back. Even though she kept her eyes fixed firmly on the path ahead of her, she couldn't help wondering what life would have been like if the man at the table hadn't jilted her, and the boy sharing the table had been hers. How much happier she'd be if she had the family she'd always wanted.

Chapter Four

"Put your dishes in the sink," Rick said, halting Bobby middash. Bobby had practically swallowed his cereal whole in his rush to get away. Rick tried not to take his son's rejection personally, but understanding didn't take away the sting. It was hard to reconcile this kid with the one who'd been his best bud from the moment they'd met. "Don't go far. We've got a lot of cleaning to get done. The furniture is arriving Monday."

Bobby huffed out a loud breath then grabbed his bowl and cup and dropped them into the sink with a loud clatter. Lucky for him nothing broke. Not that the dishes were all that expensive. It was the attitude that was getting on Rick's last nerve. And wasn't that phrase a blast from the past. He now knew what his mother meant when she'd said those words about him years ago. He was going to apologize to her for everything he'd done wrong the next time he spoke to her, whenever that was. His younger sister had taken over the family business four years ago, and ever since then his parents had been traveling like the retired people they were. They were currently on a nine-month cruise around the world.

Grabbing his basketball, Bobby went through the house, each step punctuated by the thud of the ball bouncing off the floor. Rick gritted his teeth, determined not to say anything. He didn't want all of their interactions to be confrontational. Last night at dinner was the first time in a while that Bobby had smiled. He'd almost been his old self. He'd seemed awed—and bewildered—by Charlotte. Rick could definitely relate to the bewilderment. When she'd said goodbye, Bobby had a goofy, love-struck grin on his face. Rick wondered if his son had developed his first crush.

Any other time and with any other woman, Rick would have found Bobby's crush amusing. Not now. Charlotte might have eaten dinner with them last night, but he didn't kid himself that they'd put the past behind them. Bobby might be gung ho about establishing a relationship with Charlotte, but Rick knew she didn't feel the same. Bobby had been rejected and hurt enough. Rick didn't want Charlotte adding to that pain, even inadvertently.

He heard the front door slam shut as he was taking his last swallow of coffee. The thump of the basketball pounding against the driveway soon followed. Rick glanced at the clock as he headed for the front door. He couldn't imagine Charlotte would be happy about being awakened before seven o'clock on a Saturday morning. He opened the door and stepped into the warm North Carolina morning. "Stop with the ball. You'll wake up Charlotte."

"No, I won't," Bobby protested. "She's already awake."

Rick descended the stairs and crossed the grass.

Charlotte's garage door was up and she was checking the air in her rear bicycle tire. She looked up but didn't speak before turning back to the pump.

"I hope Bobby didn't disturb you with his basketball," Rick said. Dressed in pink shorts that hit her midthigh and a pink-and-white-striped shirt, she was definitely disturbing him. She pushed to her feet and he got an even better view of her long, toned legs.

Her brown eyes were bright and sharp with intelligence. Her honey-brown skin was clear and glowed with good health. Her cheekbones were high and her full lips were enticing in their perfection.

"He didn't." She wheeled out her bike then lowered her garage door.

"Hey, are you going for a ride now? I'm not doing anything, so I'll come with you." Bobby abandoned his ball in the middle of the driveway and raced toward their garage. "Dad, open the door so I can get out my bike."

"I told you we have work to do around here."

"All I do is work. I had to pack up our old house then clean it up. Now you're making me clean up this house so I can unpack the same junk. You never let me have any fun. Why did you bring my bike if you're never going to let me ride it?"

"Charlotte didn't invite you."

Bobby turned hopeful eyes to Charlotte. Yep, that was puppy love Rick saw in his son's eyes. "It's all right with you if I come, isn't it?"

Charlotte's face didn't give anything away. That was a change from the girl he used to be able to read like a book. But back then she'd only had one page. Whatever her dad wanted was what she did. Now she seemed to have developed the ability to keep her feelings from showing on her face. "I ride fast."

"I'm fast. Aren't I, Dad. I can probably ride faster than you."

"I'm riding a long way. I'm going to the beach and riding on the sand, which isn't easy. You need strong muscles in order to do that."

Bobby pumped up his chest. "I am strong. I carried those heavy boxes yesterday plus I helped bring in our beds. And I can ride a long time." He shifted from one foot to the other. "Come on, Dad. Open the door."

"I can tell him no if you want to go alone." Rick made the whispered offer despite knowing how disappointed Bobby would be.

Charlotte looked at Bobby, who was holding his breath, his face revealing his anxiety. Her lips turned down but Rick could tell she was weakening. She nodded once. "Fine. This time."

Bobby grinned.

"Okay. I'll be right back," Rick said, following his son.

He opened the garage door. Bobby wheeled out his bike and then Rick did the same. He'd loaded their bikes at the last minute, hoping he and Bobby could do something fun that would draw them closer again. Rick didn't want to let the opportunity slip away. They could clean later.

"What are you doing?" Charlotte asked when Rick rode up beside her. She'd accepted his apology and even eaten dinner with him, but clearly she hadn't forgiven him. Not that he blamed her for holding a grudge.

"You said you didn't mind company." Under other circumstances he wouldn't foist himself on her, but this was a chance to get closer to Bobby. And who knew, maybe he would be able to show Charlotte how much he regretted his past behavior, that he wasn't the same person he'd been back then.

Her lips twisted and her eyes narrowed, but she still looked ridiculously sexy. "I said *Bobby* could come."

"Yeah, Dad, she said I could come. We don't want you hanging around us."

Rick froze. He knew his son was lashing out because he was in pain, but that didn't make the rejection hurt any less. Rick met Charlotte's eyes. There was some emotion there, but before he could figure out what it was, she blinked and it was gone.

"Oh, for pity's sake," she snapped, "let's just go." She pressed her pedals and shot down the driveway, Bobby not far behind.

She wasn't kidding when she said she rode fast. Good thing he was in shape. Even so, it took him two blocks to close the distance between them. Their speed didn't allow them time to talk, but it didn't hinder him in checking out her spectacular body and the way her round bottom looked on the seat of her bike.

After about a mile, Bobby began to fall back and Rick slowed. Charlotte had been adamant about not adjusting her pace in order to suit them, so he was surprised when she slowed as well. Not enough that Bobby would notice and take a hit to his ego, but enough for them to catch up to her at the entrance to the beach. She stopped and stood with her legs on either side of the bike. "You're a great rider, Bobby."

His son beamed and stood a little taller. "Thanks. Are we going to ride on the sand? I've never done that before."

"Yep."

Bobby gave a cheer and his smile broadened. Incredibly, Charlotte had managed to get smiles out of his son without really trying. Maybe she'd be able to help him get Bobby back on the right track, since nothing he tried was working. But that was if she would agree to spending time with them, something he seriously doubted.

"Stay away from the edge of the water. The damp sand is murder to get through." With that Charlotte once more began pedaling furiously. She set a good pace as they rode, but he had the feeling she was going more slowly than usual in deference to Bobby. Words couldn't express how grateful he was to her for that simple kindness. It was such a sharp contrast to the way Bobby's mother had walked away without giving him a second thought.

After about twenty minutes Charlotte made a U-turn and they started back across the beach. She didn't stop when they came to the entrance, but rather sped onto the road. Then she slowed, and she and Bobby rode side by side. The wind carried their voices but Rick couldn't make out the words. Once they laughed and he was filled with envy. To his shame he was jealous that Charlotte had established a rapport with his son that he'd lost. She'd gotten more smiles out of Bobby today than he'd managed in months. Worse, he envied his son for making Charlotte smile, something he had yet to do.

When they arrived home, they pulled into Charlotte's driveway and hopped off their bikes. She unlocked her garage door and started to raise it.

"That was fun," Bobby said, running to help Charlotte. "Thanks for letting me come."

"Sure." She smiled. "I guess you need to help your father clean up before your furniture gets here. See you later."

Bobby sighed and Rick waited for the explosion. It

didn't come. Instead, Bobby nodded. Grinned. "Yeah. See you later."

Rick tossed Bobby their keys. "Unlock the door and put up your bike. I'll be there in a minute. I need to talk to Charlotte."

Charlotte stiffened, but didn't speak until Bobby was out of earshot. "We don't have anything to talk about."

"I just wanted to thank you for letting us come with you. I know you would have preferred to go alone."

"I didn't mind Bobby's company."

He tried not to wince at her direct hit. "Got it. Well, thanks. You made Bobby's day."

She turned and vanished inside her garage, pulling the door down behind her. He turned away from the closed door and pasted on a smile before he went to join his son.

Charlotte sat on her patio, staring into her coffee and trying to beat back the guilt that poked her conscience. No matter how hard she tried to block it out, she kept seeing the hurt on Rick's face when she'd told him he was a nuisance. Okay, so she hadn't said it in so many words, but her meaning had been unmistakable. Naturally she didn't want him hanging around, but she didn't have to be nasty about it. Especially since she'd allowed him to accompany her on her ride. He'd known he and Bobby had intruded and he'd been trying to be polite. In the blink of an eye she'd turned into the horrible person she was sick of being. A person she'd vowed to stop being.

She exhaled, but the guilt stayed with her. Now she owed Rick an apology. Unlike him, she wouldn't wait twelve years to deliver it.

The sound of a large truck rumbling down her street

yanked her away from her musings. Air brakes sounded followed by the slam of doors. Rick's movers had arrived. Her quiet morning over, she walked to the front of her house just as Rick emerged from his door and spoke briefly with the men. A moment later there was chaos. Organized chaos, but chaos nonetheless.

Bobby spotted her and raced over. Apparently they were now best pals. He was one of a few. She frowned and forced herself to face the truth. He was one of one.

"Can I hang out with you?"

"Don't you want to tell the movers where you want your stuff?"

"As if Dad will let me. He said I could decide where I put my bed, but the next thing I knew, he was saying I couldn't put it in the middle of the room. He made me put it against a wall." His eyes flashed with anger and he frowned.

"Did you really want it in the middle?"

"Yeah. Wouldn't you?"

"Nope. If you put it against the wall, it's easier to shove stuff under it when you have to clean your room."

He smiled. "I didn't think of that. Where should I put the dresser?"

"I don't know. It depends on the layout of the room. You know, like where the door is and the windows and closet."

He rubbed his thumb over his nose. He hung his head a little although she couldn't imagine why. "So there is a right place for things to be?"

"Not necessarily. You can put your furniture the way you like it best. It's just putting it in a certain place will make it more convenient for you."

"My mom always did things like that."

"Oh?"

"She liked it. She liked buying pillows and lamps and stuff. And clothes. Dad used to tell her to stop spending money on so much useless junk, but she would just buy stuff and hide it. Then she would pretend she'd had it for a long time."

Charlotte wouldn't touch that wearing a hazmat suit. "Okay. Well, the next time you talk to her you can ask her for advice."

His shoulders slumped so much he looked like a turtle going into his shell. "I don't know how to talk to her. She left and never came back."

Oh, no. Poor kid. "When?"

"A long time ago." He sniffed. "She doesn't want to be my mom anymore."

"Then she's a fool. You're a great kid."

He looked at Charlotte in surprise, then wiped his arm across his eyes. She saw the tears but knew better than to comment on them. She would hate having anyone witness her break down. As far as people knew, she was made of stone. Everyone knew stone didn't cry.

"How come you aren't at work?"

He'd shared his hurt. It was only fair that she do the same. "I used to work for my father's company. I did everything he wanted. Not just at work, either. All the time. Last week, the day you moved to town, he gave the job I worked hard to get to someone else. So I quit."

"Wow. Did you yell and throw stuff?"

She had to smile. "No. I just stood up and left the meeting."

"Why didn't he give you the job? Is it because you're a girl?"

Was it? Maybe. But she had no control over that. "No. I think it's because he doesn't love me. Not really."

Bobby grabbed her hand with his grubby one. "Then he's a fool, too."

Charlotte's heart lifted as she looked at Bobby, his words helping her to see what she had a hard time believing. The problem wasn't with her. She was lovable. If only to a ten-year-old boy.

Chapter Five

Charlotte leaned back in her lawn chair and closed her eyes, basking in the quiet evening. She'd gotten used to living next to an empty house, so the earlier commotion had been a change. It wasn't necessarily a bad change. Just noisy. The movers had driven away in the large truck, taking the smaller truck Rick had driven with them. Before coming outside, she'd heard bumping as Rick and Bobby continued to move things around. They finally stopped an hour ago when Bobby had protested loudly enough for her to hear.

She couldn't believe Rick Tyler was not only in Sweet Briar, but living next door to her. Unbelievably he was still trying to be friends. Didn't he know leaving a woman standing in a church dressed in her wedding gown ruined the relationship for all time? Did he think he could charm his way back into her good graces? She wasn't that gullible. Or forgiving. Of course, every time he saw her he apologized. He was sincere, but that wasn't enough for her to forget that he'd humiliated her in front of every person she knew.

He was attractive, but not that attractive. Okay, so he was sexier than he'd been a dozen years ago. He'd been handsome then but now he was off-the-charts gorgeous. Tall, dark and handsome might be cliché, but only if the description didn't apply. And it definitely applied to Rick Tyler. His dimpled smile was almost beautiful enough to make her forget the past. Almost.

"I was hoping I'd find you out here."

Charlotte didn't turn at the sound of Rick's voice although she did open her eyes and watch as he crossed his lawn and hopped over the rosebushes separating their properties. Without waiting for an invitation, he dropped into the chair beside her. He had two unopened bottles of water. He offered her one, which she took even though she wasn't thirsty. He twisted the top off his and took a deep swallow.

"What are you doing here?" She'd apologized to him for being rude the other day but that didn't mean she was ready to bury the hatchet. There was too much pain between them for that. She was simply trying to become a better person.

"In Sweet Briar or in your backyard?"

"Either. Both."

He stretched his long legs in front of him and crossed one ankle over the other. "I'm in Sweet Briar because I'm opening a medical practice here. I told you."

"Cut the crap. You can open a practice anywhere. Why come to my town?"

He sighed. "You're different. The Charlotte I remember would never have pressed me like this."

"It's amazing what being made a laughingstock in front of an entire town can do to a young girl's personality. It cures that eager-to-please disease permanently, leaving no chance for relapse."

"I'm sorry—"

She cut him off. "I don't want to talk about that ever again. The past is over and I survived. We were discussing your sudden desire to live in a small town. Specifically this small town."

"A couple of reasons. First I really like Sweet Briar. I liked walking down the street and seeing familiar faces. Friendly faces. I want that for Bobby. Of course, I know I have to prove that I'm reliable. I imagine my reputation is not the best after I stood you up at the altar."

She raised a hand, stopping him. She didn't need to rehash the past. She'd lived it. "You said a couple of reasons. What's the other one?"

"You."

"Me?" She wasn't sure she wanted to hear this.

"I wasn't happy with the way I left things between us. You deserved better."

"So you moved here as some sort of penance? You could have just apologized in an email."

He winced. "An apology is only part of it. I want to try and make amends."

"That's not necessary."

"I'm a better person."

"You don't have to prove that to me."

"Maybe I need to prove it to myself."

She didn't want to talk about Rick anymore, but suddenly she didn't want to be alone, either. Most of her life she'd been alone. And lonely. She searched for another topic. "Bobby told me he hasn't seen his mother in a long time."

Rick leaned forward, his elbows on his knees, his hands clasped. "It's been a year and a half. Our divorce was final about six months before that. I wanted joint custody but she didn't. She didn't want anything to do with him. I begged her to see him and even offered her more money in the settlement. I thought I'd convinced her to stay in his life, but I was wrong. She took the money and ran."

"I don't understand how a mother can just leave her child." Her heart still ached for Bobby.

"That makes two of us. Sometimes I wonder how long she'd been planning it. I don't know if she really loved me or if she was just looking for a way out."

"A way out of what?"

"Motherhood."

"I don't follow you."

"Bobby didn't tell you?"

"Tell me what?"

"I'm not his biological father. I met Sherry when he was six. We married shortly after that. A couple of years later she was gone, leaving him behind."

Although she was relieved that Rick hadn't immediately married another woman and had a child after he left her, she was furious at the cruel way Bobby had been treated. "I'm the last person to pretend to know what perfect parenting looks like, but I know that isn't it."

"Bobby's been having a hard time."

"Do you blame him?"

"No. I understand. But I can't excuse his behavior. He stopped doing his schoolwork and became disruptive in class. Then he started hanging out with some bad kids and getting into more trouble. I had to do something. Moving across the country might be drastic, but I'm desperate."

"And you think living in Sweet Briar will provide

some magical cure? I've got news for you. We have bad kids here, too."

"I'm not expecting miracles although one would be nice. I was working a lot of hours before and didn't have the time to devote to him. My practice here will be slower, so I won't be as busy. I'll be able to hang out with him. He lives and breathes basketball. Maybe there's a league he can join. I'll even coach."

"That might help. But what about his mother?"

"What about her?"

"What if she decides she wants to see him again?"

"She won't."

"You never know. Maybe she was depressed or over-whelmed." Charlotte knew she was reaching, but she couldn't fathom a woman walking away from her own kid. Especially one as great as Bobby. There had to be something wrong with that woman.

"She wasn't depressed. She met someone and was starting her life over without any baggage—her word, not mine—from the past. She told me she didn't want him and if I didn't take him she'd put him in foster care."

"Ouch."

"Yeah. That's another reason we needed to move. Even though he denied it, Bobby was still hoping Sherry would come back."

"And you?"

"Me? Definitely not. My love died a long time ago."

"Okay. That tells me why you're in Sweet Briar. But why are you in my backyard?"

"Because it's where you are."

"Don't be flip. I'm serious."

"I didn't realize I was being flip. I wanted to talk to you and you were out here."

She turned to get a better look at him. Unfortunately,

a cloud moved in front of the moon, extinguishing the little bit of light in her yard. A citronella candle flickered on the table, but it provided minimal illumination. Although she would have preferred to see his expressions in order to better judge his veracity, this might be better. After all, he wouldn't be able to see her face, either. "That's just it. Why do you want to talk to me?"

"We always talked in the past. I could always count on you to understand what I meant without having to go into great detail."

"That was then. When we were friends. Or at least I thought we were. We aren't friends now."

He sat up, uncrossing his ankles. "What do you mean you *thought* we were friends?"

"Friends don't hang each other out to dry. Friends don't leave friends to face the most embarrassing situation of their life all alone." She told herself to keep calm, but her voice rose anyway. "Do you have any idea what that day was like for me? How humiliated I felt?"

"It didn't have to be that way. Remember I asked you to go with me to tell our parents we didn't want to get married. You refused. I know now I could have handled things differently, but at the time I had no idea how. To be honest, I still don't know what else I could have done."

"You could have come to the church."

"And done what? Are you saying you were going to stand up to your father at the church when you weren't willing to do so before?"

"I don't know. Probably not."

Rick grabbed her hand and gave it a gentle squeeze. "I'm sorry for embarrassing you, but calling off the wedding was for the best. I don't know everything about marriage, but I know it won't work when the people aren't in love. And we weren't."

"Speak for yourself. You might not have been in love with me, but I was in love with you. That's why I didn't want to call it off."

Charlotte had been in love with him? How could he have not known that?

"Good night." Charlotte stood. "Blow out the candle before you leave."

Rick jumped to his feet, blocking her path. "Wait a minute. You can't drop a bombshell like that and just rush off. We need to talk about this."

"There's nothing more to say. I loved you. You didn't love me back. The end." Charlotte stepped around him and sprinted into her house, leaving him alone. He dropped back into his chair, his mind reeling. How could he have been so blind?

Sure, Charlotte had never discussed her feelings. Neither had he. He'd cared about her, sure. And been wildly attracted to her. At another time and place in his life he might have fallen in love with her. But he hadn't been ready to be a husband with all the responsibility that came with marriage. He didn't want to be trapped and unable to follow his dream of becoming a doctor.

He still couldn't believe how fast things had spiraled out of control back then. He'd known Charles Shields was controlling, but his own normally levelheaded father had shocked him. His dad had gotten swept up in the idea of doing business with Shields Manufacturing, turning his own successful business into a mini-empire that could support his wife and seven children in grand style, and had temporarily lost his way.

Rick closed his eyes, wishing he could close his mind to the pain in Charlotte's voice. She'd loved him. And he'd repeatedly told her they weren't in love and didn't have to marry. How could he have missed it? The only excuse he had was that he'd been young. And she had never once told him.

Rick blew out a breath. The past was over. He couldn't go back and change things, so there was no use continuing to think about what he could have done differently. He just needed to do better in the present.

Charlotte appeared incredibly isolated. Where was the man in her life? If she had one, Rick would have seen him by now. And what about friends? Rick had overheard Charlotte tell Bobby she quit her job. Shouldn't her friends have shown up with a pizza and a six-pack by now? Or chocolate and wine? Or whatever it was that women used to drown their sorrows. Yet not one person had.

The Charlotte he remembered had been sweet and funny, if a little reserved. Had she changed that much? And how much of that was his fault? No matter. He'd liked the girl Charlotte had been and he really liked the woman she'd become, prickles and all. He had to find a way to get her to forgive him.

Grabbing the empty water bottles, he crossed the lawn and went into his house, stepping around boxes. He had to get his house in order in more ways than one.

Chapter Six

Why in the world had she told Rick she'd been in love with him? For years she'd kept her true feelings to herself, letting everyone believe she'd only agreed to marry him because she'd thought it made good business sense. That had made her look cold and emotionless, but that was certainly better than having the entire town know the man she'd loved hadn't loved her back. That he'd thought nothing about how she'd feel when he didn't show up at the church. That her heart had shattered into millions of pieces and still hadn't mended.

Although he'd told her he didn't want to get married, she hadn't thought he was heartless enough to leave her standing there all alone. She'd remained at the church long after everyone had gone. When she'd finally faced the truth, she'd taken off her dress, button by button. She'd briefly considered burning it, then decided to keep it as a reminder of how much pain she was in. She never wanted to forget just how agonizing love could be.

She'd loved Rick with her whole heart and soul. Marrying him would have been a dream come true. She'd scribbled embarrassing notes in her diary about how happy they were going to be together. She'd sketched designs of their house and garden. Heck, she'd even named their kids. The future she'd planned was going to be so much better than the life she'd lived before he'd come along. And he hadn't had a clue how she'd felt until she'd opened her big mouth last night.

Rick was the last person she'd wanted to know how devastated she'd been. Now when he looked at her it would be with pity instead of respect. That was something she couldn't handle.

She pedaled faster and harder, blinking the sweat from her eyes. Her muscles screamed yet she didn't slow her pace. Maybe if she wore herself out she would be able to erase the image of Rick's shocked face from her mind.

She turned and began riding home. The sun, which had been struggling to make its way across the horizon when she'd started out, was now shining in the sky. Exhaustion nearly claimed her as she coasted into her garage. Legs wobbling, she headed upstairs for a long shower. Maybe that would wash the memories of last night from her mind.

Fresh from the shower, Charlotte pulled on a floral sundress and white strappy sandals. Sitting at her makeup table, she ran a comb through her hair, making sure every strand was in place. She put on her favorite dangly crystal earrings before brushing on mascara and lip gloss. She always took care to look nice, but she put a little bit more effort into her grooming this morning.

She would have preferred to spend the day alone, but that wasn't possible. She'd promised to help Bobby arrange his room. Of course, that was before her loose lips had sunk her pride. Still, she wouldn't let him down. With a mother who'd abandoned him without a second thought, he'd experienced more than his share of disappointment. She wouldn't pile on more. So she'd suck it up and look Rick in his gorgeous eyes without blinking. She was tough enough to survive his knowing her deepest secret.

After eating a breakfast of boiled egg whites and a bowl of mixed fruit, she turned on her computer. She'd given herself a week to get over the hurt and shock of her father appointing someone else as president of Shields Manufacturing. It was time to put that betrayal behind her and get on with her life. She needed to update her résumé and get it out to headhunters. Although she had saved enough money to live comfortably for a while, she didn't want to spend the next few months twiddling her thumbs while her bank account dwindled. She liked working and the sense of accomplishment that came from doing a job well and knowing she was a contributing member of society.

Although she'd worked for her father's company her entire career, she'd held a variety of positions. She'd started at the bottom and worked her way up. Years ago, Rick had tried to convince her to get a job with another company, just to get a different perspective. She'd thought he was nuts. The idea of letting someone else benefit from her education had seemed more than disloyal. It was blasphemous. Too bad she hadn't known her loyalty was a one-way street.

She printed out the draft of her résumé and set it on her desk. She'd review it later and then send it out and see what kind of interest it garnered. One thing was certain. She was leaving Sweet Briar. She'd gotten into a rut here, and didn't see a way out. She didn't have any friends and she'd made plenty of enemies. Although she wanted to start over, her reputation would always be in the way. And since she'd earned it by being cruel and rude to just about everyone in town, there was no one to blame but herself. There would be no clean slate in Sweet Briar.

But if she moved to a different state, one where no one knew her, she could start over fresh. Her past, including her failed wedding, would truly be a thing of the past. Rick's presence would no doubt stir up gossip, but knowing she was leaving soon would make it bearable.

Her doorbell rang, putting an end to her thoughts.

"You ready, Charlotte?" Bobby asked as soon as she opened the door. He was grinning from ear to ear.

"Yes." She grabbed her keys and locked the door behind her.

Bobby led the way, smashing two of her flowers in his excitement. There was a time when that would have bothered her, but what the heck? Did she really need the perfect lawn and perfect flowers?

"Most of my stuff is piled in the middle of the room," Bobby said as he held his front door for her. "I told Dad not to touch anything."

"Really? How did he take that order?"

"He just kind of laughed. Probably because I told him you were going to be in charge."

Or maybe he laughed because he thought she was using Bobby to try to get close to him. She nearly snorted. The last thing she was trying to do was get Rick back. Heck, he moved to her town, not the other way around. If everything worked out it wouldn't be her town much longer.

"I'm not in charge," she corrected him as she followed him up the stairs.

"I'm not letting Dad be the boss," Bobby said, folding his arms across his skinny chest.

"Hold on. I'm not saying your dad is in charge, either."

"Then who?"

"You. This is your room. I'm here to help. I might make a few suggestions, but the final decisions will be yours."

"Really?"

"Yes."

"But you'll help. I don't want to do anything stupid."

"I'll help. And don't worry about doing anything stupid. There is no such thing."

He stopped at a closed door, turned the knob and began to push. Ever so slowly the door opened enough for them to squeeze through. Boxes and bags were scattered around the room willy-nilly. The bed was against the far wall and was what passed for made in a ten-year-old's world. The comforter had been pulled up, but a thin blanket peeked from beneath it, dragging the floor. The big lump in the middle was no doubt a pillow. A dresser, desk and chair were in the middle of the floor.

Wow.

Bobby looked at her expectantly. "Where should we start?"

"By opening the window. If we can make a path and get over there. It's kind of stuffy in here."

"No problem." Bobby twisted and contorted his body around boxes and stepped into a basket that she hoped was dirty clothes, finally reaching the window. He unlocked and opened it, then turned to her, a look of triumph on his face. "What next?"

"Where's your dad?"

"Right behind you."

Charlotte jumped, wondering how Rick had sneaked up on her like that. Somehow he'd managed to open the door wide enough to get inside. With his broad shoulders that was no easy thing. Of course, he had muscles to spare, so maybe it was easy. He stepped closer and she got a whiff of aftershave mingled with his natural scent.

"I didn't see you standing there," she said inanely.

His grin would be better suited to a pirate than a family practitioner and single father. "I'm at your service. What do you need?"

"Another pair of strong arms to help move boxes and furniture."

"We don't need him," Bobby said, rushing forward, knocking over a plastic bin in his haste to get to her side. Dozens of cases of video games spilled across the floor but he ignored them. He smiled at her, then glared at his father. "We can do it by ourselves."

Rick's smile faded in the face of rejection. A meaner, pettier version of herself would have been happy that he was getting some of his own medicine, but instead she felt sad for him. He loved his son and Bobby was shredding Rick's heart without even knowing it. "Speak for yourself, Hercules. If you notice, I'm not exactly dressed for moving boxes. Nor are my muscles as big as yours and your father's. No. I think I'll take a seat on the throne and direct you two peasants. You may bow at my feet now."

Bobby's brow wrinkled in confusion and he blinked a couple of times. After a moment, he grinned and swept into an awkward bow. "Okay, your queenliness."

"And don't you forget it." She raised an eyebrow at

Rick, who was staring at her and Bobby, an unreadable expression on his face. "You may bow as well, peasant."

He grinned and seemed to get into the mood. His bow was decidedly more graceful than his son's. He took her hand and kissed it, sending chills down her spine. "I'm your servant, your queenliness."

Her cheeks grew warm and she hoped he couldn't see her blush. Bobby somehow managed to carry his chair to her without knocking over anything. She busied herself straightening her dress before she sat down.

"What should we do now?" Bobby asked.

She looked from his eager expression to Rick's amused one. Darn, he'd noticed that he'd flustered her. "I think we should get the clothes put away. That way we can clear out some of these boxes. Are you going to set up your game system in here or somewhere else?"

"In here," Bobby said immediately.

"In the living room," Rick replied, just as quickly.

"Okay." She wasn't going to get into the middle of that debate. "You two decide on that later."

"There's nothing to decide," Rick said firmly. "The system will stay in the living room like before."

Bobby narrowed his eyes and folded his arms over his chest in typical kid anger. This fun time was rapidly turning into a battle of testosterone.

"I like to play," she said, playing peacemaker. "I might invite myself to come over and play with you. It would be easier if the games were downstairs so we could sit on the couch."

"We could sit on my bed."

Charlotte laughed. "Sorry, Bobby. I don't think your dad would appreciate you having girls in your room."

"You're not a girl. At least not the kind of girl Dad means."

"Let's put the game system downstairs. That way you can have all kinds of girls over." Charlotte was trying to sound reasonable even as she tried not to look at Rick. She could only imagine what type of girl he thought she was. The desperate kind.

"Okay. But I'm not going to have girls over. Just boys. If I ever make any friends here. I haven't seen anything but old people."

"Like me?"

He nodded. "And the mayor. I bet there aren't any kids in this stupid town."

"You'd lose that bet. There are plenty of kids here. They hang out at the youth center. Your dad can take you there. You'll make friends in no time."

Bobby took a deep breath and Charlotte got the feeling he was about to launch into another tirade about his dad, so she cut him off at the pass. "Okay. Let's move this dresser to the wall next to the closet. I think it works better there."

"Okay."

Bobby pushed against the dresser. It was solid cherry, so it didn't budge.

"That looks like a job for two people," Charlotte pointed out. "And the queen doesn't move furniture."

Rick sauntered across the room. "I can't do it alone, but if we work together we can move it."

Charlotte's heart warmed at the way Rick offered his assistance without fracturing his son's ego. Rick leaned into the dresser and grunted a little. Bobby mimicked his father's stance. Together they managed to get the heavy piece of furniture to the place she'd chosen. Bobby's breathing was heavy, but he was smiling.

"What next?" Rick asked.

Charlotte pointed to the desk and chair. After they

were moved to the place of Bobby's choosing, they began emptying boxes. "Let's hang up the clothes. We can start with the long-sleeved shirts. I'll separate them by color once they're on hangers."

"You're going to hang up shirts by sleeve length?" Rick asked, shaking his head in disbelief. "And color?"

"Why can't I just shove them in the drawers?" Bobby asked, his expression mirroring his father's.

"Never mind. I'll take care of the clothes," she said, shooing them away. They just stood there looking at her like she was crazy until she clapped her hands. "Start emptying the boxes."

She opened a box labeled Clothes. From the looks of it, Bobby had simply dumped everything in without rhyme or reason. Sighing, she began pulling out his underwear, piling underpants and undershirts beside her. She held up a pair of rolled socks. "Which drawer?"

Bobby shrugged and shot his father a confused look before turning his attention back to her. "Any drawer, I guess."

She decided to make an executive decision and organize the clothes in a way that made sense to her. She would give him a good start even though she doubted it would last.

While she worked, Bobby gathered his video games. He could have put them back into the empty plastic bin, but he grabbed them in an unruly pile that kept shifting and sliding from his arms. Using his chin and chest, he managed to keep them from falling as he left the room. She didn't comment, glad that the fight over the placement of the game system had been resolved without further explosion.

Unfortunately, his absence left her alone with Rick and her imagination. She needed to make sure he knew she wasn't still in love with him, but she didn't want to have that discussion now.

"Thanks for helping Bobby. Given our past, I don't imagine you planned on getting this involved with us."

She dropped a stack of white undershirts into a drawer then leaned her hip against the dresser and crossed her arms. "If you know that then why do you keep pulling me in?"

He looked flustered if only for a second. "To be honest, I didn't realize how badly I'd hurt you before we talked last night. I knew you were angry but it hadn't occurred to me that you were also heartbroken. I'm ashamed to admit it never crossed my mind that you'd been in love with me."

Because loving her had never been a possibility for him. She raised her hands, determined to stop him. "We don't need to rehash the past. I loved you then. I had twelve years to let the feeling die. It did." It had been a slow and painful death that left more than a few scars, but that was something he didn't need to know.

"I'm sorry for being dense and not knowing how badly I messed up."

"Fine. But know this. We're not going to be friends. We live next door to each other, so we'll see each other. We'll even speak to each other. But that'll be the extent of our relationship."

He was shaking his head even as the words were coming out of her mouth. "No."

"What do you mean no? You can't make me be your friend."

"I mean exchanging greetings isn't going to cut it." He looked up to the ceiling as if seeking answers from the cheap, ugly light fixture that needed to be replaced, then sighed. "You and Bobby have hit it off. He's been spiraling since Sherry left. You're the first person who has been able to reach him. So though you may hate my guts, I'm not taking no for an answer. Bobby needs you, so you're stuck with me."

Shocked by his bold declaration, his arrogance, she sputtered. "I don't think so. Your problems are yours, not mine. If you're having trouble with Bobby you're going to have to figure it out without me."

"Don't you like me?"

Charlotte spun around. The sad look on Bobby's face broke her heart. She might not have much use for Rick, but there was no way she could hurt this child. His mother had already turned her back on him. She couldn't live with herself if she did the same. "Yes, Bobby. I like you a lot. It's your father who gets on my nerves."

Bobby smiled and blew out a breath. "He gets on my nerves, too. But he's hardly ever around, so you don't have to worry about seeing him when we hang out."

Although Charlotte returned Bobby's smile, she knew it wasn't going to be that easy.

Chapter Seven

Rick tied twine around the bundle of cardboard boxes and shoved them into the recycling bin. He'd worked hard the last two days to get the house in shape. Or as organized as he could manage with an uncooperative kid who fought him at every turn and random thoughts about Charlotte that popped into his mind at the worst times. Every thought was accompanied by guilt. Ever since she'd admitted to having loved him all those years ago, his guilt grew. It was bad enough knowing he'd humiliated her. But knowing he'd broken her heart? That was enough to bring him to his knees.

She was so different from the quiet and unassuming girl he remembered. Now she was prickly with some hard edges and he wondered how much of her attitude was a result of his careless treatment of her. But no matter how cool she was to him, she was soft as a marshmallow with Bobby.

The day after she'd made it abundantly clear she didn't

want to be around Rick, Bobby had insisted on inviting Charlotte over to play video games. He'd become
upset when Rick said she might not want to come. Bobby
couldn't believe Charlotte didn't want to spend every
second of her day with him. While Rick had been getting his own bedroom in order, Bobby had sneaked next
door. Two hours later Rick had come downstairs to find
Charlotte with a controller in her hand. She'd been losing
the game, but she was laughing and, incredibly enough,
talking trash.

She was so beautiful. Goofing around with Bobby,
she'd looked carefree and young. The frown lines around
her mouth had eased, and she didn't have the pinched and
unhappy look he'd seen too often on her face. Something
inside him had stirred and awakened and he realized
it was attraction. He was attracted to Charlotte again.

As he thought back on it, he shook his head in disgust. The timing couldn't be worse. He had a son who
was barely speaking to him and who only let him hang
around because he didn't have a choice. Sherry had ruined more than her relationship with Bobby. She'd ruined
Rick's relationship with their son as well. He'd spent the
past year and a half trying to restore that relationship, but
so far nothing had worked.

Charlotte was the only person who'd managed to reach
Bobby. Perhaps because they'd both been rejected and
abandoned by someone who was supposed to love them.
Someone they should have been able to rely on. His stomach seized. He was one of the people Charlotte should
have been able to count on. True, her father had hurt her,
but Rick knew he wasn't blameless, either.

What a mess. He'd been confronted by screwed-up
situations many times in his life but nothing of this magnitude. At least not of his own making. His father had

anointed him his successor to the business even though Rick hadn't wanted any part of it. Their relationship had been strained for over a year as his father tried to bend Rick to his will. Rick had remained firm and in the end his father had accepted his decision. Their relationship was once again strong. If he could fix that mess, he certainly could fix this one.

And she might not know it yet, but Charlotte needed him. Not to rescue her, but to add fun and joy to her life. It seemed to him that she had lost the ability to enjoy herself and had forgotten how to laugh. He and Bobby could help with that. They needed Charlotte, but she needed them, too. Maybe they could help each other.

The doorbell rang just as Charlotte finished wiping her kitchen counter. She tossed the sponge into the sink and walked slowly to the door. She had no doubt that one of the Tyler men was standing on her porch. Although she had told Rick she didn't want him in her life, he hadn't yet caught on to the fact that she meant it. Instead, he kept coming around as if trying to wear her down. She might consider slamming the door in his face, but he knew she wouldn't do the same to Bobby. So he always brought Bobby with him.

"Are you home, Charlotte?" Bobby yelled as he rang the doorbell again. She'd asked him not to hold his finger down on it, but he either didn't remember or didn't understand just how annoying the repeated ringing was.

"I'm coming," she called. How had she become his best friend? Didn't he know nobody liked her? She opened the door and stepped outside. "What's up?"

"Do you want to come over and play? You're never going to get good if you don't practice."

She swallowed a smile. He seemed so sincere. Part

of her believed he wanted her to become better because that was important to him. Another part believed he was lonely, a feeling she knew all too well. Sure, she could hang out with him, but he needed friends his own age. Not only that, she planned to leave Sweet Briar soon. It wouldn't be fair to let him become attached to her. She didn't want him to feel like she'd deserted him when she left. And she was leaving.

"I have a better idea. There are lots of kids in town who hang out at the youth center. It's a good place to make friends. Your dad can take you there today."

"He's busy."

"Doing what?" The words were out of her mouth before she could call them back.

He shrugged and twisted his foot on the floor, making his gym shoe squeak. "I don't know. Something to do with his job."

"Let's go talk to him so we can get an idea when he can take you."

Rick was in his office when they arrived. His eyebrows rose when he saw her and a gleam lit his eyes. He lifted a finger signaling them to wait a minute, spoke into the phone, then scribbled a note on a piece of paper. "Thanks for your help," he said, then ended the call.

"We need to talk," Charlotte said.

"I told Bobby not to bother you."

"He isn't bothering me. Bobby is always welcome in my home."

"Told you." Bobby frowned. Obviously they had discussed Bobby's growing attachment to her. Was Rick trying to help her maintain the distance she wanted? If so, he was going about it the wrong way. Making Bobby feel unwanted wasn't the way to help him get over being abandoned.

"Then what do we need to discuss?"

"Bobby needs friends his age. You need to get him involved at the youth center so he can meet other kids."

Rick looked at her for a minute then picked up his car keys. "Fine. Let's go."

"You don't need me," she said, backing out of the room. No way did she want to be trapped in a car with him. She was having a hard enough time maintaining her emotional distance from across the room. If she was close enough to inhale his scent with every breath, close enough to feel the heat radiating from his body, her resolve might weaken. Then where would she be? It was only memories of blinding pain that kept her from being swept away by his charm. Even so, she didn't know how long she could hold up the wall around her heart.

"Don't you want to go with us?" Bobby asked. Oh, she was going to have to find a way to resist this kid. The pleading expression on his face only reminded her of her futile attempts to gain her father's love and attention.

"Yeah, don't you want to go with us?" Rick mimicked, closing the distance between them. His smile was wicked and way too sexy for her comfort. Clearly he was up to something but she had no idea what. Whatever it was, she wasn't going to fall for it. Now if only her body would line up behind her brain and make that tingling sensation racing down her spine vanish.

She looked away, but not before seeing the mischief dancing in Rick's eyes. She directed her response to his son. "You don't need me."

"Yes, I do," Bobby admitted quietly. His little-boy vulnerability squeezed her heart, dissolving the last of her resistance.

"Okay. I'll come."

Bobby grinned and raced out the door to Rick's car. Rick and Charlotte followed at a more sedate pace. After buckling into the seat beside Rick, she gave directions to the youth center.

Twenty minutes later they pulled into the parking lot. A vibrant mural covered the outside of the building.

"Wow. That's cool," Bobby said.

"My sister's an artist. She designed it and a lot of people helped paint it." Pride filled her although she didn't know why. Her youngest sister, Carmen, had spearheaded the effort, but Charlotte hadn't helped. She and Carmen had been estranged for years. To her shame, she'd brushed aside every overture Carmen had made. She'd ignored every phone call and had publicly snubbed her. Finally her sister had gotten the message and had moved on with her life.

"Which one?" Rick asked, reminding her that he'd spent time with her family.

"Carmen."

"Really? It's impressive."

Several young girls hopped out of an SUV and raced to the front door, followed by a smiling woman about Charlotte's age. She didn't recognize the woman. Perhaps she was one of the new people who'd moved to town in the past few years.

"How is she?"

Charlotte pretended not to hear Rick's question. How could she explain the rift she'd created with her sister? Charlotte wished things were different, but it was too late. Carmen had created a new family that didn't include Charlotte.

Rick had always been close to his big, boisterous family. Although she'd only visited their New Jersey home a couple of times, she'd easily picked up on how loving they were. There had been laughing and teasing like nothing she'd ever experienced. The Tylers and the Shieldses couldn't have been more different. She would have traded her family for his any day.

"I'm not sure how things work here," she said as they climbed the stairs.

"You haven't been here before?" Bobby asked. "Then how do you know this is a good place?"

"I have been here before," she said calmly. "And I know the people are good. I wouldn't bring you anyplace where they weren't. But I don't have any kids, so I don't know the procedures. Okay?"

He nodded. "Okay."

"Can I help you?"

Charlotte turned. A woman in her early twenties seated behind a large desk beamed at Rick and Bobby. When she turned to Charlotte, her smile faded. Charlotte saw the question on Rick's face but ignored it. "I'm Charlotte Shields. This is Dr. Rick Tyler and his son, Bobby. They've just moved to town and Bobby is interested in participating in activities here."

"Welcome." The young woman focused on Rick and fluttered her eyelashes. Her smile magically reappeared. She was way too young to be interested in a man his age, but that didn't stop her from flirting. Charlotte wanted to tell the girl to knock it off. The thought irritated her. Why should she care who fawned over Rick? He wasn't her fiancé any longer. They weren't even friends. Still, someone should tell this girl it was unbecoming to come on to a man in front of his son.

"We'll just need to get some information on you and your son, Doctor." The girl attached two papers to a clipboard and handed it to Rick. He grabbed the pen dangling from the clipboard by a string and completed the forms.

"If you want, I can get someone to cover the desk for me so I can show you around."

"No, thanks," Charlotte said, pasting a smile onto her face. She'd had enough. "I'm familiar with the layout. I'll show them around."

Before the girl could object, Charlotte led the way through the building. The walls were covered with beautiful murals that could only be more of her sister's work. The paintings were bright and exuberant and filled with joy. Just like Carmen. An ache the size of an ocean grew inside Charlotte when she thought of the distance she'd put between herself and her baby sister. She didn't kid herself that there was a way to bridge that divide. She'd torched those bridges long ago.

When their father kicked Carmen out of the house, Charlotte had been an adult with a home of her own. She hadn't invited her sister to stay with her. Instead, she'd sided with their father, turning her back as well. When Carmen returned two years ago to attend their mother's funeral, Charlotte had been terrible to her, going so far as to publicly humiliate her sister.

The sound of laughter filled the air and they followed it to the gym. Ten or so boys around Bobby's age were standing in a circle. From the looks of it, they were choosing teams for a game. One of the boys looked up. "Hey."

Bobby looked at Charlotte, a question in his eyes. She smiled and nodded encouragingly. "Hey," he answered although he remained by her side.

"Do you play basketball? We need one more person."

Apparently those were the magic words because Bobby unfroze and raced across the gym. The adult leader said something Charlotte couldn't hear that made the kids laugh. A couple of minutes later the kids grabbed red or blue vests and put them over their T-shirts. Bobby flashed Charlotte a grin then joined the other boys wearing blue vests on the far side of the gym.

The adult leader turned and walked in their direction. Charlotte's stomach sank. It was chief of police Trent Knight. Her brother-in-law. Although he was never outwardly hostile to her—as the chief of police he couldn't be and perform his duties properly—he was definitely not friendly. Of course, since his first loyalty was to Carmen, Charlotte didn't fault him. She'd always hoped to be first with someone, too. Life just hadn't turned out that way.

Trent extended his hand to Rick and the two men introduced themselves. Trent nodded at Charlotte and she returned the gesture. Again Rick looked puzzled but he didn't say anything. No doubt he was waiting until he had her alone to bombard her with questions.

"So you're the new doctor. Welcome. I can't tell you how glad we are to have a doctor in town again."

"I'm glad to be of service."

The kids began calling Trent's name. "I'm the referee, so I had better get to it. Stop by the police station anytime and we can have a cup of coffee."

"Sounds good. What time should I pick up Bobby?"

"Whatever time suits you. We have the gym for two more hours before the older kids come in. We'll probably grab some snacks and head to the game room. If he gets bored or wants to leave, he can give you a call and you can pick him up. How's that?"

"Sounds fine."

Rick didn't speak as they walked back through the youth center and to the car. After they fastened their seat belts, he turned to her instead of starting the car. "What's going on here, Charlotte?"

"What do you mean?"

He blew out an exasperated breath. "Really? You're going to pretend not to know what I'm talking about? Fine. Why is everyone treating you like you broke their favorite toy and then laughed about it? Why are people so rude to you? The receptionist. The police chief. Why?"

"Not everyone is popular. Some people are in the in-crowd and others aren't."

"There's more to this behavior than cliques. This is flat-out hostility."

"Just let it go. I don't want to talk about it with you." Or with anyone.

He studied her, frowning. Finally he nodded, but she knew this wouldn't be the end of it. He was just coming up with a different strategy. But just how was she supposed to explain that in seeking her father's approval she'd turned the entire town against her? And that the father she'd devoted her life to hadn't contacted her once since she'd quit her job. She'd finally broken down and called him, but he'd refused to speak to her. She shouldn't have been surprised. He hadn't spoken a word to Carmen or even mentioned her name in years. When Charles Shields cut you out of his life, it was permanent. She just couldn't believe he'd do it to her. Or how much it would hurt.

The minute Rick pulled into the driveway, Charlotte bolted from the car and vanished behind her door. He could make a nuisance of himself and follow her, but he decided against it. Stubborn as she was, she would remain as tight-lipped as she'd been on the drive home.

He needed a different way to discover why people were so rude to her.

He'd promised to leave it alone and he would. For now. But if she thought he would sit back and do nothing while she was mistreated, she had another think coming. He'd let her down before. He would never do it again.

With Bobby at the youth center, Rick had several hours of uninterrupted time. He stopped at the hardware store for paint. Although he needed paint for both the house and his practice, he would focus on the medical building first.

After deliberating for a few minutes, he settled on a calm pale blue for the exam rooms and an equally relaxing yellow for the reception area and waiting room. A middle-aged man was leaning against the counter of the paint mixing area, talking with an apron-clad, toothpick-chewing employee. They stopped talking as he approached.

"What can I do you for?" the employee asked, a wide smile on his face. His name tag identified him as Harvey.

"I need paint."

"Then you've come to the right place."

Rick showed him the chips. "I need ten gallons of each."

"That's a lot of paint." Harvey looked at him searchingly.

"You must have a big job to do," the other man added.

Rick smothered a smile. He'd forgotten how inquisitive people in small towns could be. And how much everyone enjoyed being the first to know something. "I'm Rick Tyler, the new doctor in town. I'm going to be painting my offices."

"You don't say." Harvey swiveled the toothpick from one corner of his mouth to the other. "That's a pretty big job. If you want help, I can recommend some college kids who do a pretty decent job. And they don't charge all that much."

"That might work. I could use one or two guys. How do I get in touch with them?"

"Joseph Whitfield and Brady Edwards work at the youth center. You can leave messages for them there or here with me and I'll get in contact with them for you. Just let me know when you want them and they'll be there."

"Thanks. I'll do that."

"Hey, I remember you," the other man said as he gave Rick the once-over. "You were engaged to Charlotte Shields. You left her standing at the altar."

Rick's mind spun as he sought to find words to explain his behavior and to assure them that he was not the irresponsible person he'd been a dozen years ago.

To Rick's surprise, the men laughed and Harvey's friend patted his back. "I don't blame you for running. You really dodged a bullet there."

"You can say that again," Harvey added. "That Charlotte Shields went to school with my youngest daughter. She's a piece a work. Believe me, no one in town thinks you were wrong. If anything, people wonder why you proposed in the first place. Lucky for you she showed her true colors before it was too late."

The men stared at him as if they expected him to join in and trash Charlotte as well. Or perhaps they were waiting for more details about why he didn't show that they could spread around town. Either way, they were going to be disappointed. "I didn't leave Charlotte standing at the altar because she was a horrible person.

I did it because I was a jerk. She deserved better than that. She deserved better than me."

They stared at him, their mouths agape, too stunned to reply. Rick paid for his paint, tape and tarps and walked out of the store. As he drove the short distance from the hardware store to his office, he breathed deeply, trying to calm his anger. Men old enough to be his father were actually gleeful at Charlotte's suffering. How many other people in town felt that way?

What Charlotte had endured for the past twelve years was even worse than what he'd imagined. He had more to make up to her than he'd thought.

Calling himself all kinds of names, he taped the woodwork and laid out the tarps. As he spackled the tiny holes in the wall, he tried to come up with a plan, but he was too upset to think straight.

After a couple of hours, he decided to pick up Bobby. This was his first time at the center and he didn't want him to feel like he'd been dumped and forgotten. Bobby was starting to relax and Rick didn't want to make a mistake and mess that up.

"Hello, Doctor," the young woman at the reception said, straightening in her seat and running a hand over her hair. "How can I help you?"

"I'm here to get my son."

"Okay. I think he's in the game room. If you'll sign him out I can have someone get him."

"Thanks." He scrawled his name where she indicated, then stepped away from the desk. The girl was attractive and he was picking up on her signals, but he wasn't interested. She was way too young for him. Besides, he didn't have space in his life for a woman now. Bobby needed all of his attention.

The sound of thundering feet stirred him from his

musing as Bobby raced through the hall, sliding to a stop inches in front of Rick. A smile lit his young face. "Why are you here so early?"

"It's your first day. I wanted to be sure you were having a good time."

"It's great here. Just like Charlotte said." He looked around. "Where is she?"

"I took her home. She had things to do and so did I." Which reminded him. "I need to leave a note for a couple of kids. Then we need to get going. You can come back tomorrow if you want."

"I want to come back every day."

Rick scratched out messages for Brady and Joseph and left them with the receptionist, who promised to make sure the boys received them. He only hoped she didn't take the liberty of copying his phone number for her own personal use.

Bobby bounded out the door and into the car.

"So what did you do?" Rick asked as they drove home.

"Everything. First we played basketball. We won the first game but the other team won the second. The coach said it was all in fun so nobody got mad. Then we had lunch. We had hot dogs and chips. They made us eat vegetables. I tried to tell the lady I gave them up for Lent but she only laughed and gave me some carrots. She put dip on them so they weren't so bad." He turned in his seat. "Why don't you ever put dip on my vegetables? They aren't so nasty that way."

"We can do that."

"Maybe we can tell Charlotte so she can try. Then she can be strong like us. Well, maybe not as strong since she's a girl, but stronger than other girls."

"Sure." Rick definitely wanted to be around when

someone told Charlotte she couldn't be as strong as a boy. Of course, since she liked Bobby she'd probably let him get away with it.

"Me and Nathaniel played video games for a little while."

"Nathaniel and I," Rick corrected him automatically. "And who is Nathaniel?"

"My friend. He told me his mom's sick, so I told him you were a doctor and could make her better."

Rick grunted noncommittally since he didn't know anything about Nathaniel's mom. Bobby kept talking, making further response unnecessary. "We're going to hang out tomorrow. If it doesn't rain we're playing baseball. I told Mr. Knight that basketball is my favorite, but they want kids to play outside, too. Oh, there's a trip to the beach coming up. I need your permission. Nathaniel told me he went to a ranch and rode a horse a couple weeks ago. He said the man let him ride all by himself and he went fast. I want to do that. Can I go next time?"

"I don't know. Was it a field trip?"

Bobby shrugged. "I don't know. I'll ask Nathaniel tomorrow. He doesn't have a game system, so I told him he could come over and play with me."

"If it's okay with his mom, we can set something up."

"She's sick, remember? His uncle lives with them, so Nathaniel's going to ask him."

"Sure." Rick wasn't sure how he would pull off everything Bobby wanted, but he would do his best. Bobby was more enthusiastic than he'd been since Sherry left. "Did you get his phone number?"

"No. And I don't have a phone anyway." He shot Rick a meaningful look. The battle for a cell phone had recently flared up and Bobby was attacking whenever he saw an opening. Though Bobby was determined, Rick intended to win this battle. A ten-year-old didn't need a phone. Rick didn't reply. They were home anyway, ending the conversation for the time being.

Bobby hopped out the car and headed for Charlotte's door.

"Where are you going?"

"I want to tell Charlotte about today."

"Maybe you should wait until another time. She might be busy."

"She told me she's never too busy for me."

That was a surprise. "Really?"

"Yep. She likes me."

Rick followed his son up the stairs. He wouldn't mind seeing Charlotte again. Despite knowing there was no space in his life for a woman, there was something about her that drew him. She'd been much nicer and more accommodating when they were younger, but he found the mature version more appealing. Or maybe he had grown up enough to truly see her inner beauty and appreciate her strength. Not that it mattered. Bobby needed to be the center of his life. Even knowing that, his heart leaped in his chest when Charlotte opened the door and smiled.

Chapter Eight

She and Rick needed to talk. He obviously hadn't gotten the message last time. Or the times before that. Perhaps she hadn't been clear. Odd. Generally people understood what she meant the first time. Of course, she'd been dealing with subordinates and had been less than diplomatic, not something she was proud of now. She didn't want to bring that harshness to her personal life. But still, she needed to make sure Rick got the message this time.

He couldn't keep coming around. Being neighbors didn't make them friends. Their lives were separate. He was the one who'd wanted it that way. She'd wanted to marry him but his plans hadn't included her. Now her plans didn't include him. But every time she turned around, there he was.

Like two days ago. She'd expected Bobby to come over and tell her about his day at the youth center. After all, she'd recommended it. But she hadn't anticipated

Rick showing up with his son. She'd tried to focus on Bobby, but she hadn't been able to ignore the way Rick's casual shirt clung to his muscular torso. Or the masculine scent that surrounded her whenever he leaned in close, or the light in his eyes when he laughed at something Bobby said.

So, yes, they very definitely needed to talk.

"Oh, good. You're home."

Had she conjured him up just by thinking of him? Because there he was in all of his masculine glory, standing on her patio beside the bag of mulch. He looked better in his paint-stained T-shirt and basketball shorts than most men did in a tailored suit. She'd never admit that to him, though.

"There's no fooling you."

"I need a favor."

"And yet you came to the one person guaranteed to tell you no. You look so much smarter than that." Actually, he looked sexy, but that information was need-to-know and he didn't.

"It won't take long," he continued as if she hadn't just shot him down. "Maybe an hour or so. And you'll be saving my life."

The charming smile he flashed made her heart go pitter-patter, which only annoyed her. She refused to be attracted to him. "Actually, since you're probably the last person I'd do a favor for, it won't take a minute. And as for saving your life... Need I say more?"

He sighed and his broad shoulders slumped. "You're never going to forgive me. I get it now. I kept hoping that you would relent, that you would see me as the man I am now, but you're not going to. Don't worry—I won't bother you again. I'll let Bobby keep visiting you. I just won't accompany him."

Her heart plummeted to her feet, shocking her. Wasn't this what she wanted? Hadn't she been planning to tell Rick to leave her alone?

Leave her alone. "Alone" definitely described her. She'd rebuffed every offer of friendship that had ever come her way. Was she going to run off another person seeking to become a part of her life? How much more was she willing to sacrifice on the altar of pride?

And really, just what did she want Rick to do? How many apologies did she need before she forgave him? Or did she intend to hold on to her anger until she became a bitter, unforgiving old woman? A lonely, friendless old woman.

"Wait."

Rick paused, but kept his back to her. For a moment she wondered whether he would turn or walk away. Maybe it was too late. Finally he spun around. "What?"

This was the moment of truth. Could she actually forgive him? Once she said the words, there would be no going back. She blew out a breath. Incredibly she felt relief at the idea. She was ready to release the anger that had held her captive for most of her adult life. "I accept your apology. I know I said it before, but this time I mean it. I forgive you."

Just saying the words was like a weight was lifted from her shoulders. No, from her heart. Forgiveness really was freeing. She felt so liberated she said it again. "I forgive you, Rick."

He looked at her speculatively, as if he wasn't sure she meant it. "Really?"

She smiled. "Really. So what did you want?"

He grinned sheepishly. "I'm going to the grocery store and I'd like adult company."

"Why do you need company at the grocery store, of

all places? Scared of getting kidnapped by a lonely and desperate woman?"

He laughed and shook his head. "I really hate that sense of déjà vu."

She couldn't help but ask. "Déjà vu?"

"You know. Wasn't I just here pushing this cart? Didn't I just buy bread? And milk?"

Charlotte laughed. "I know what you mean. I put it off as long as I can. You've seen my pantry. Old Mother Hubbard has nothing on me. I need to go shopping myself."

Rick hesitated as if afraid to push his luck. "The thing is, I'm not only shopping for me and Bobby. I'm holding an open house to let people see my practice and I'm not sure what to serve. I thought you might provide a bit of guidance. And you can pick up your groceries at the same time. It's a win-win."

She looked down at her clothes, which were a little dirty from gardening. "I'm not dressed to go out."

His eyes swept over her body, and darn, didn't that crazy fizzy feeling grow in her stomach. He lifted one corner of his mouth. "You look fine to me. Who dresses up to go grocery shopping?"

A Shields did. Children of Charles Shields represented him wherever they went and should never be dressed in less than their best. But then, she was no longer obligated to please anyone other than herself. She took off her gardening gloves and brushed her hands over her shorts. "Let me get my purse."

Rick checked the time then opened the door. Although he wasn't going to officially open his practice until Monday, he was holding an open house today so the people of Sweet Briar could meet him. He hadn't hired a nurse yet but he'd scheduled interviews for to-morrow. Two of the candidates looked promising. He'd hired a receptionist-slash-file-clerk who was starting tomorrow. Things were moving right along.

Several people were milling around waiting outside. He smiled and stepped out of the doorway, letting everyone enter. "Welcome. I'm Rick Tyler."

"I'm Joni Danielson," the first person to come in said. She was a pretty woman with a bright smile on her face. "We haven't met yet. I'm the director of the youth center."

He grinned. "My son, Bobby, has mentioned you often. You're becoming one of his favorite people. Next to his best friend, Nathaniel."

"He's a great kid. Very enthusiastic."

"Thanks. Look around. Get yourself an appetizer and some punch. Maybe we can get together and talk later. Bobby has mentioned a couple of upcoming field trips and I'd like to get the details if you have time."

"I do."

She continued inside and another person followed her. Rick shook many hands. Some people he remembered from the past, some he didn't. He hoped they'd give him the opportunity to provide them with good health care. He handed out business cards listing the office number and hours. Flyers with the same information were stacked on the reception desk as well.

Each time the bell over the door rang, he looked up, hoping to see Charlotte. Each time he was disappointed. She knew about the open house. He'd placed his food order the day they'd gone grocery shopping. She'd been in favor of the stuffed mushrooms and pinwheel sandwiches. Somehow she'd convinced him to get a fruit platter instead of a vegetable tray, claiming no one would eat the carrots and broccoli. Despite how well they'd gotten along, he hadn't managed to get her to promise to come today.

The open house lasted two hours. When the last person left, he closed the door and leaned against it. Though it seemed most of the town had attended, it hurt that Charlotte hadn't bothered to stop by. Telling himself to get over his disappointment, he pushed away. He'd taken a step when there was a knock on the door and the knob turned.

"Am I too late?" Charlotte asked, poking her head inside.

His heart leaped in his chest as he opened the door. "Not at all. Thanks for coming."

"I almost didn't come."

"What changed your mind?"

"I remembered that I'd forgiven you. Since I'm no longer holding a grudge, I was free to see your office." She smiled as if what she'd said made perfect sense.

Dressed in a black-and-white sundress and white sandals, she looked like a dream. Smiling, he took her arm and led her inside. As she passed by, her floral scent wafted around him, tempting him to pull her near. His arms ached to hold her close, but he'd forfeited that right long ago. Besides, she was more likely to slug him than return his embrace.

She turned slowly, looking around. "I love the way this waiting room looks. You chose a great wall color and you did a great job painting. The chairs look really comfortable. Why do you have a television? Planning on keeping people waiting a long time?"

"No. But it's a good way to keep waiting family members occupied. Especially kids. I'll have some books and magazines, too, but as a father I know nothing occupies a kid like watching TV."

"True."

"Let me show you the rest of the place," he said, putting his hand on her waist. She jumped slightly but didn't move away. She felt warm beneath his touch and his palm tingled. Bypassing the reception area, he led her into the first examination room. There was a scale by the open window and a breeze blew through, gently moving the blinds. A table was against one wall, ready for the first patients. The stainless-steel sink glistened.

"Nice. Again, I love the colors you chose. Very soothing."

"Thanks."

Charlotte walked out the room and he followed. After showing her the other examination room, he led her to his office. The desk and guest chair took up most of the small space, so they had to stand close together. The warmth from her body drew him to her. He looked into her eyes. They were so clear. So open. So beautiful.

He wanted to kiss her. As he moved closer, she blinked and stepped back, bumping into the desk. The sparkle in her eyes had dimmed and she gave him a bland smile. He thought she might say something about what had almost happened but she didn't. Apparently she was going to pretend she didn't feel the same pull he did. That was fair, he supposed, given how badly he'd hurt her. But still, her behavior was contrary to everything he was discovering about her. Charlotte was no shrinking violet. She was strong. Direct. She didn't pull her punches.

Or was that an act? Had she become so adept at putting up barriers to protect herself from the pain of rejection? His chest ached as he contemplated that his thoughtlessness had caused her so much pain. He'd gotten what he'd wanted at great cost to her.

"Well." Charlotte rubbed her hands together, looking over his shoulder. "Thanks for showing me around. I'm sure you'll be busy in no time."

She started for the exit and he stepped in front of her. She was retreating, turning into the remote woman she'd been before. No way was he going to allow that to happen. They'd made progress in their relationship and he wasn't going to move backward. "Surely you aren't going to leave me with this mess to clean up."

"Actually, I am."

"That's not at all neighborly. What will Bobby say when I tell him you didn't help at all?"

She laughed. "You're kidding, right? He'll definitely take my side."

"True. You can do no wrong in his eyes."

"However. Since I want him to learn how to be a true friend, I'll lend a hand."

"Thanks."

"But just one. I'll take care of the food and gather up the cups and saucers. You'll have to handle everything else."

"Deal."

Cleaning with Charlotte was nice. She didn't talk but rather went about her task with an efficiency that was astounding. And he couldn't keep his eyes off her. He was drawn to her beauty and the gentleness that existed beneath the hard exterior she showed the world. Every once in a while her softness peeked out. Maybe if she was treated with kindness, her softness would appear regularly.

"I'm done," Charlotte said, breaking into his musings.

"Me, too. I just need to tie the garbage bag and put it in the dumpster. Wait a minute and we can walk out together."

He hurried off before she could find an excuse to leave. "How about lunch?" he asked when he returned.

"How can you be hungry? You had a ton of food."

"I was busy talking to everyone, so I didn't eat. Most of the town showed up."

"That's good."

"So how about lunch?"

"What about Bobby?"

"He's at the youth center. You were right about that place, by the way. He loves it. He's already made a best friend. Since he likes to spend most of the day there, it's just you and me. How about Heaven on Earth? I've heard the food there is great."

A cloud passed over her face and her look of uncertainty had him hoping she wouldn't say no.

"If you would rather go somewhere else, we can do that. I just thought you might like something a little nicer. And you look so beautiful in that dress it would be a shame to waste it on the diner. But we can go there if you prefer."

Her spine straightened. "No. Heaven on Earth will be fine. And you heard right. The food there is delicious."

Charlotte looked around the restaurant and expelled a pent-up breath. Although most of the tables were filled, she and Rick had managed to snag a good table in a quiet corner. Not that any table could be considered bad. Far from it. Brandon Danielson was talented, and not just in the kitchen. He'd designed the room so that no table, even those placed in corners, felt cramped. No, it wasn't the restaurant causing her unease.

"So what's good?" Rick asked, putting down his menu.

Charlotte looked away from the other diners and focused on the printed page. She'd only eaten here a couple of times, and those had been business dinners. Brandon's sister, Joni, waitressed for Brandon from time to time, so Charlotte preferred not to dine here. Joni was Carmen's best friend and didn't like Charlotte. Not that she had ever come out and said so. She was too classy for that. Whenever they met she was unfailingly polite. She just didn't treat Charlotte as warmly as she did every other person in town. Of course, since Charlotte hadn't gone out of her way to be friendly, either, she couldn't hold Joni's attitude against her.

"I thought you knew about the food."

"Only that it's good. What do you like, Charlotte?" Rick put his hand on hers, brushing his thumb over the back of her hand.

Distracted, she blurted out the first thing she thought of. "Paella."

He raised an eyebrow. "Really? I thought you didn't like shrimp."

How did he remember that? It had been a throwaway comment made years ago. Despite herself, she was pleased he remembered. "Not for me. For you. I know you like shrimp."

"All seafood. Okay. I'll try that. What are you going to get?"

"I'll try the chicken stuffed crepes." She slipped her hand from under his. She couldn't think with him touching her.

They placed their orders with the waitress who smiled broadly at Rick and nodded stiffly at Charlotte. Charlotte didn't recognize the woman, not that it mattered. Her reputation preceded her. Over the years she'd told herself that she didn't care how much she was disliked and that small-minded jealous people couldn't hurt her. She'd lied. Every snub, no matter how well deserved, hurt. Unfortunately, it was too late to change things in Sweet Briar. She wouldn't make the same mistakes in the future.

In her new town, nobody would know anything about her. They wouldn't know she'd been abandoned by her fiancé on her wedding day. She wouldn't be a laughing-stock, or worse, an object of pity. Nor would she have to live up to her father's impossible standards. She wouldn't be an unfriendly snob. She could just be plain old Charlotte Therese Shields. Whoever that was.

After the waitress walked away, Rick placed his arm on the table and leaned in close. Even after all this time she recognized the intensity in his eyes. He was about to start a serious conversation. One she was sure she didn't want to have.

"What's going on?"

"I don't know what you mean." Technically that was the truth. His question was broad enough to encompass any number of topics.

"With that waitress. Do you know her? She was borderline rude to you. I have half a mind to complain."

"Don't do that."

"Why not? Did you have some sort of conflict with her?"

"Are you serious?"

"You bet I am."

He sounded more than serious. He was furious. On her behalf. Her heart skipped a beat. She'd never had an advocate before, someone willing to take on the world for her. She'd always had to fight her own battles. If necessary she still could. But taking on the world was tiring. Still, this wasn't a battle worth fighting. Especially for Rick. She'd be gone soon, but he was making Sweet Briar his home. He didn't need to make enemies by defending her.

"There's no conflict."

"Then what's with her attitude?"

"You really don't know?"

"No."

He hadn't been in town long, so it was possible no one had told him. She wasn't vain enough to think that she was the subject of every conversation. Still, she didn't want him to know how badly she'd alienated everyone. Oh, he'd find out eventually, of that she was certain. But he wouldn't hear about it from her. "It's really nothing, Rick. You're an attractive man. Even a woman having a horrible day would find time to flirt with you. Me, not so much."

He didn't seem convinced, but thankfully he let the matter drop and they chatted about inconsequential matters until their food arrived. He waited until she took a bite of her crepe before lifting a forkful of paella to his mouth. The expression on his face was pure bliss.

"Wow. This is the best thing I've eaten in my entire life."

"Better than half-baked chicken and black rice?"

Rick laughed so hard she thought he would choke. "I wasn't going to mention that meal."

During the early days of their relationship, Charlotte had attempted to prepare a romantic dinner in order to impress Rick. The chicken had been bloody and the white rice had burned. Calling the meal a disaster would have been generous.

She laughed with him. "That was my first attempt at cooking a meal. Charmaine was the one who liked hanging out in the kitchen with our mother. I planned on being the tycoon and taking over the family business. My skills are only marginally better now. Lucky for me there are more restaurants in town than there were twelve years ago. Otherwise I'd starve."

"In other words, I shouldn't come to your house hungry."

"You can come. Just be prepared to leave the same way."

"Fair enough. But I can cook. I needed to learn in order to keep Bobby fed. Feel free to come over anytime you want a home-cooked meal."

"I'll keep that in mind." Not that she planned to ever act on it. Even though she'd forgiven him, they weren't friends. So why was she having such a hard time remembering that? Perhaps because she was having more fun with him than she'd had with anyone else in years. And would being friends with Rick actually be that bad? It would be nice to have a friend even for a short while.

"How's Charmaine? I thought I would have run into her by now."

Charlotte's laughter died as she thought of her younger sister. She and Charmaine were only two years apart in age, but they were as different as night and day. Where Charlotte was bold, Charmaine was quiet. Charmaine avoided conflict at all costs. Charlotte didn't enjoy fights, but she would rather be battered and bruised than run away with her tail tucked between her legs. Despite their differences, the sisters had once been close. All three of them had been. Now the gulf between them was vast, and becoming close again seemed an impossible dream. Charlotte had turned her back on her sisters, so she bore the majority of the blame. She'd been the one to burn the bridges.

"She doesn't live here. She moved to Florida last year to take a teaching position." Something that had shocked Charlotte. She hadn't known about Charmaine's plans until she'd received an email with Charmaine's new telephone number and address. Charmaine had probably thought Charlotte would tell their father if she'd known in advance. Sadly that was true. Charlotte had turned everyone in her family against her. All to get the love of a man who didn't care about any of his daughters. Carmen and Charmaine had stopped trying to win Charles's love long ago. Only Charlotte had kept beating her head against the impenetrable walls of his heart.

"Good for her. What about Carmen?"

"She still lives in town. I told you that. Remember she painted the murals at the youth center."

"Oh, yeah."

"She's married to the chief of police and has two stepdaughters."

He shook his head. "I can't believe Carmen is all grown up. In my mind she's still the little girl who followed you everywhere, trying to do everything you did."

"Time passes so fast. If you blink you can miss a year." Taking all the opportunities to reconcile with it.

"What are your plans now that you no longer work for your father?"

"I have three telephone interviews scheduled for later this week. If things go well, I'll move on to in-person interviews."

"Wow. You're not letting moss grow under your feet."

"I'm not much for downtime."

"I remember that about you. You didn't like to waste time even when we were dating."

"I just don't like being idle. I enjoy the challenge of finding solutions to problems."

He nodded. "I can't disagree with that. I love being a doctor."

"I bet you're good at it, too."

"I hope so. But don't make the mistake I did and focus so much on your career that the rest of your life suffers. My marriage fell apart. Maybe she never loved me. I'll never know. But my relationship with Bobby suffered and I'm still trying to restore it. Make time for friends and romance."

When she moved to her new town she'd make time for friends. But romance? Not on your life. No one was going to slice her heart into pieces again, including the handsome man across from her who was even more appealing now than he'd been when they were engaged.

Chapter Nine

Rick wrote the last note, then closed the patient's file. Although he had an updated computer system that made billing insurance companies easier, he preferred to keep written notes as well. Grabbing the folder, he headed to the front of the office, where Marla, his receptionist, was shutting down her computer.

She looked up and smiled at him. "I just made another appointment for next Friday. You're booked for the entire week."

"It helps to have a monopoly. Right now people are just feeling me out. The real test will be when someone gets sick. Will they come and see me then?"

"I wouldn't worry if I were you. Everyone has been more than satisfied. You're going to be treating the entire town in no time."

"That would be nice." He'd seen quite a few people since he opened the office on Monday. He'd envisioned it taking a while to get his practice up and running, so this was a nice surprise. This was further proof that moving to Sweet Briar had been the right thing to do.

Marla opened the bottom desk drawer, pulled out her oversize purse and slipped the strap over her shoulder. "Have a great weekend. I'll see you Monday."

"Thanks. You have a good weekend, too."

After locking up, he drove to the youth center to pick up Bobby. Although Bobby would stay until closing if he could, Rick liked to eat dinner together and then do something fun in the evening. He wanted Bobby to be happy here, and he was. But that was only part of the equation. They needed to rebuild their relationship and that required spending quality time together.

Bobby jogged to the reception area accompanied by a boy about his age. "This is Nathaniel."

"Hi. It's nice to meet you, Nathaniel."

"Are you going to make my mom better, Dr. Tyler?"

"Has she come to see me?"

"Not yet. She always goes to the hospital in Durham. But now that you're here she won't need to go so far."

"Okay. She's welcome to come see me. But remember she might like her other doctor better."

"They don't know what they're doing. They aren't making her better."

Rick wasn't sure what to say to that, so he only nodded.

Nathaniel turned his attention to a man who was coming inside and grinned. "Hi, Uncle Paul."

The other man smiled. "Hey."

"This is my friend Bobby and this is his dad. His dad is a doctor."

The other man extended a hand. "Nice to meet you."

"He's going to make Mom better."

"I only told Nathaniel she was welcome to come and see me," Rick said, hastening to correct the youngster.

Paul looked at Nathaniel. "Why don't you go get your sisters."

"I'll go with him," Bobby offered. The two boys turned and raced down the hall.

"Sorry about that," Paul said.

"No worries. Bobby already mentioned that Nathaniel's mother is sick."

"Cancer."

"I don't want to be inappropriate and discuss her medical care or health with you."

"You're not. To be honest, most of the time I'm lost trying to understand what the doctors are saying. Not to mention being worried."

"I can imagine. I'd be going nuts if one of my sisters was so sick."

"Sister-in-law."

"Oh."

"My half brother ran out on her years ago and she doesn't have any other family. She reached out to me when she got too sick to care for the kids."

Rick handed the man a card. "Feel free to call me if you have any questions. I'm in family practice but I have lots of contacts. If I don't know the answers I can get them for you."

"Thanks. I appreciate it."

Bobby and Nathaniel returned with two cute little girls who Rick guessed were Nathaniel's sisters. Each of them carried a clay sculpture with the reverence normally reserved for works of the great masters. One was a yellow butterfly with pink spots and the other a blue bird with a red breast.

"Look what we made, Uncle Paul," the bigger girl said as they lifted their projects higher.

He admired each one. "They're beautiful."

"They're for Mommy."

"She's going to love them."

"Mrs. Knight made stands for us to put them on. Nathaniel has them."

Nathaniel held up the two carved blocks of wood. Each one was stained and had a brass plate on the front. Rick was too far away to read the words engraved on them.

"That was nice of her. Come on. We'd better get going."

"Can Nathaniel come over to my house tomorrow?" Bobby asked.

"It's no problem," Rick added.

"Okay."

"What about us?" the older girl asked. "We want to come."

"I thought you wanted to go to Amy's birthday party," Paul said.

"Oh, yeah. Never mind."

Rick watched as Paul led his charges out the door. The man had a lot of weight on his shoulders, but he carried it well. Bobby started to follow the group out. "Hold on. I want to talk to someone."

Bobby nodded. "Okay."

Rick asked the receptionist for directions to the art room and was escorted there by a young man who looked like he could bench-press an SUV. He was friendly, though, engaging Bobby in conversation about basketball.

Apparently the kids were finished for the day because a young man was dipping a cloth into a bucket of soapy water and scrubbing dried paint from a long table. A woman was seated behind a desk, cutting strips of newspaper and dropping them into a basket. Soft music played from a DVD player on the corner of the crowded desk.

The young man looked up. Rick recognized him as Joseph Whitfield, one of the youths he'd hired to paint his office. "Hey, Doc. Are you looking for Bobby?"

Rick shook his head. "Actually, I was looking for Mrs. Knight."

"That's me," the woman said, looking up. A confused expression crossed her face and he could tell the minute she recognized him. "Rick."

He blew out a breath. Another person he needed to mend fences with. That was why he'd sought her out. He knew how close she and Charlotte had been years ago, so he'd expected her anger. Knowing he deserved it didn't make it any more palatable.

Joseph dropped the rag into the bucket, splashing suds onto the table. He moved to stand beside Carmen, the smile on his face replaced with a look of concern. Tension radiated from every pore in the kid's body. Clearly Carmen had a protector.

"I recently moved to town and I wanted to say hi."

"Really? After what you did you have a lot of nerve coming here."

Rick just stood there. Carmen obviously was just getting warmed up because she stood and moved around the desk. He looked at her, and despite the gravity of the conversation, he couldn't help but laugh. She was pregnant.

"What's so funny?"

"You look like you're about to pop."

She folded her arms over her enormous stomach. "Is that the way you talk to your patients, Doctor? If so, you won't last long."

He shook his head. "No. Charlotte didn't mention that you were pregnant."

"You've talked to Charlotte?"

"Of course. She's my neighbor. She's the one who told me about the youth center and that you volunteer here. Those are some great murals, by the way."

"She told you about me?"

"Yes. She's very proud of you and all that you've accomplished. According to her, you're a successful artist."

Tears filled her eyes and he wondered what he'd said wrong.

She gulped. "Charlotte told you that?"

"Yes. Why? It's not a secret, is it?"

She started to laugh.

"I'm going to call the chief," Joseph said, grabbing a cell phone from his pocket. He looked as worried and confused as Rick felt.

Carmen put a hand on his arm, stopping him. "You don't need to do that. I'm okay. I'm just a little surprised."

"Are you sure?" Joseph's hand hovered over the screen.

"Yes. Go ahead and finish cleaning the tables."

Joseph shot Rick one last threatening look, or as much of a threat that he could pack into a stare while wearing a lavender ruffled apron, then picked up the cloth and continued working. Joseph kept his eyes on Rick as he worked, ready to jump into action if Rick made one false move.

"Why are you surprised Charlotte told me about you?"

"Because she hasn't spoken to me since I moved back to town."

"What? I find that hard to believe." Twelve years ago

Charlotte had been an indulgent big sister. He couldn't imagine that changing. Then he thought of the shadows he frequently saw in her eyes. It occurred to him that although Charlotte had quit her job, Carmen hadn't come to check on her. "What did you do to her?"

"What did *I* do to *her*?" Carmen opened her mouth then closed it. She tilted her head to the side as if trying to see inside of him. "Wait a minute. What's going on between you and my sister?"

"Nothing."

"I don't think so."

"Leave it alone, Carmen." He paused. "No, don't leave it alone. Why don't you give her a call?" He wouldn't violate Charlotte's privacy, but if he could give her a confidante, he would.

"I have. Repeatedly. The next move has to be hers."

"And if she does make that effort, will you talk to her?"

"Why does any of this matter to you? You left her standing in the middle of the church in her wedding gown."

"Wow. That's messed up," Joseph said, looking at him with something akin to disgust. Rick felt even worse than he had before, if that was possible. Even a teenager knew he'd been a selfish jerk.

"Because of the way you humiliated her, she changed. She became just as mean and awful as our father. She turned her back on me. And it's all your fault."

"She's forgiven me," Rick said lamely.

"Good for you," Carmen snapped, glaring at him.

There was nothing else to say, so Rick decided to leave. "Congratulations on your pregnancy."

As he and Bobby left the center, Carmen's words kept playing in his mind. He was the cause of Charlotte's change and the reason she was estranged from her family. Her apparent lack of friends was probably due to him as well. He had a lot to make up for.

The ringing doorbell was becoming a regular part of Charlotte's day. Bobby came over every evening to tell her about what he'd been up to and Rick always concocted a reason to hang out with them. After the first couple of visits, she'd bought a bag of chocolate chip cookies and a gallon of milk. When Bobby mentioned he loved chocolate milk, she'd bought a bottle of chocolate syrup.

Today, they were a little bit late and she was worried they might not stop by. Why? When had they become so important to her? How had they managed to wiggle their way into her heart?

The doorbell rang. She exhaled the breath she'd been holding and raced to the door.

"Surprise!" Bobby yelled, yanking a bunch of roses from behind his back.

"Wow. These are beautiful. Thank you."

"Are you surprised?"

"Completely."

"It was Dad's idea. He said women like it when you bring them flowers."

She lifted the bouquet to her nose. The sweet fragrance filled her with happiness. "What brought this on?"

Rick shrugged. "Do I need a reason?"

"Most people have a reason for doing things."

"True. Then let's say it's because you're our favorite girl."

Her heart fluttered ridiculously even though she knew

he didn't mean anything by the words. Or by the flowers. He was just being nice. "I'll put these in some water."

The three of them walked into the kitchen. While she dug a vase from under the cabinet, Bobby grabbed the bag of cookies and headed for the refrigerator and milk. She hadn't lived with anyone since she'd moved out on her own. Although technically Bobby didn't live with her, he'd definitely made himself at home. So much so that he felt comfortable leaving a trail of cookie crumbs on the table and floor. And he always left his empty glass on the counter instead of putting it in the dishwasher.

"Guess what?" he asked around a mouthful of cookies.

"You have a girlfriend."

He rolled his eyes. "You're the only girl I like."

"Okay, then. I can't imagine."

"Nathaniel's coming over tomorrow. We're going to play video games all day."

"All day?"

"Yep. You can come over if you want."

"Thanks. I have a few things to do, so I don't know if I'll be able to come." She was getting too close to the Tyler men. She needed to be careful.

"I'm grilling hot dogs and burgers," Rick added as extra enticement.

He knew she loved simple foods, and burgers and hot dogs were among her favorites. Her taste in food had failed to mature; it remained adolescent. That was one of the things her father held against her. Try as he might, he couldn't change her palate. Sure, she ate the occasional sophisticated meal, but she preferred regular food that Charles considered beneath them. He'd probably lose his mind if he saw the stash of junk food she kept in her pantry, to say nothing of the handful of bite-size candy she kept in her purse because...well, just because. Her high-calorie diet was part of the reason she rode her bike religiously. That and the pleasure she derived from it.

Still, she didn't want to be too predictable. It wouldn't hurt to throw Rick for a loop. "Maybe I'll have filet mignon."

He laughed. "Okay. A burger."

"Make that two. With cheese and lots of grilled onions. And of course I'll need a hot dog."

"Done."

"Can I watch your TV?" Bobby asked, wiping his mouth on his sleeve.

"Sure. Put your glass in the dishwasher first."

He complied, then ran from the room. If she ever saw the kid walk she'd check him for a fever. Not that she knew exactly how to do that. But since his father was a doctor it wouldn't be necessary. And why was she thinking about that anyway? Things were getting out of hand. She needed to get Rick out of her house before she did something stupid like forget how badly he could hurt her.

That was the problem. She was starting to forget the pain. Once she'd truly forgiven him, her memory of the past hurt had begun to dim. Oh, she still remembered being left at the altar. That was something she'd never forget. But thinking of it no longer ripped her heart to shreds. Amazingly, the pain was fading.

He stood. "I hope you can make it tomorrow. Bobby will miss you if you don't come."

"Just Bobby?" The words burst from her lips before she could stop them. But now they were out there, hanging between them.

"Definitely not just Bobby," Rick said. "I'll miss you, too."

Her heart thudded in her chest. She didn't know what they were doing and she needed time to figure out if getting closer to Rick was a mistake. "Okay. See you tomorrow."

"Tomorrow," Rick echoed.

Charlotte wasn't sure if his reply held a threat to her heart or a promise. Either way, she knew she was walking down a path and she didn't know if she could stop.

Chapter Ten

Charlotte checked her appearance one last time. Although this was not remotely close to a date, she was a bit nervous about seeing Rick again after she'd revealed more than she'd planned to about her confusing feelings. Bobby and Nathaniel would be there, but she didn't count on them being around much. They'd either be playing computer games or shooting hoops in the driveway like they'd been doing since Nathaniel arrived an hour ago.

Deciding her red linen shorts and tan-and-red sleeveless top looked great, she touched up her lipstick and turned away from the mirror. She hadn't slept well last night. Instead, she'd replayed their conversation over and over again, hearing the echo of a promise in his words. Her hand still tingled from his touch. She didn't know if getting closer to Rick was the right thing for her, but staying away from him was a losing battle. She would have an easier time walking away from a perfectly grilled hot dog with all the works. Thankfully she would be leaving town soon, so no matter how close they got she still had an exit.

Not that she was running. She wasn't a weakling. She was being realistic about her future plans. Plans she had no intention of altering for him.

She grabbed two party-size bags of potato chips and a jar of French onion dip, her contribution to the meal, and walked across the lawn. The smell of charcoal filled the air and her stomach growled. There was nothing like charbroiled meat to soothe whatever ailed her.

Rick was bent over, filling a cooler with ice, so she took the opportunity to study him. Dressed in a gray T-shirt that clung to his muscular torso and faded jeans that emphasized his strong thighs, he looked more appetizing than a double cheeseburger and fries. Looking was fine as long as she didn't touch, so she looked her fill, then cleared her throat.

He turned and smiled. "Hey. I was wondering when you were getting here. For a minute I thought you had chickened out."

"I was slaving over a hot stove." She lifted the snacks and they laughed.

He stepped close as if to touch her and she sidestepped him. "I should put these in a bowl."

"I'll handle that. Just sit down and relax." He took the snacks from her. His hand brushed hers and she felt a spark. She extinguished it. She wasn't going to stumble down that road again.

Charlotte sank into the nearest chair, grateful for a moment alone to gather herself. The moment passed too quickly. But then, it didn't take much time to open a bag of chips and dump them into a bowl.

"How about a drink?" Rick asked as he set the snacks on the table.

"What do you have?" Charlotte asked, digging out a chip and using it to scoop up dip.

"Root beer, grape and of course cream soda."

Man, he was going all out. Those were her three favorite types of soft drinks. She couldn't believe he remembered that about her. "Grape."

He grabbed a can, popped the top and handed it to her.

She looked around the yard. The patio was spotless as if recently washed and the furniture was clearly new. The grass was freshly cut and the bushes neatly trimmed. Her previous neighbor had planted annuals every year but Rick hadn't chosen to do the same. The landscaping was a little bare as if advertising that a single man lived here. Still, she felt comfortable.

"How's the job hunt going?" After grabbing raw vegetables from a tray and dropping them on a plate, he sat down beside her.

"I had three phone interviews. Both went well. I have in-person interviews scheduled for next week."

"Which companies?"

"They aren't local. Two are in South Carolina and the other in Chicago. My headhunter is still sending out résumés all over the country, so I might not end up in either of those places."

"You're thinking about leaving Sweet Briar?"

"I'm doing more than thinking. I'm leaving."

"But why? This is your home. You grew up here. Your family is here." He sounded upset although she couldn't imagine why.

"None of those things are selling features."

He swallowed. "Is it because of me?"

"I never took you for the egotistical type. Did med

school do that to you? Maybe all those people deferring to you and calling you Doctor has gone to your head."

"That's not what I meant and you know it. Our past and present are pretty convoluted. Maybe that's not something you want to deal with."

"My plan to move doesn't have anything to do with you. Not really. I just need to start over where nobody knows me."

"I understand getting a fresh start. Bobby and I moved here for that reason."

"Then you know why it's important for me to leave."

"I would agree if I didn't think you were running away from something."

Stalling for time, she sipped some soda and tried to figure out what to say. She settled on the unvarnished truth. "In a way I guess I am."

"From what?"

"Myself."

"I hate to be the one to tell you, but that won't work. Wherever you go, there you are. It's a fact of life."

"That's not what I mean. It's just that I'm trapped here in Sweet Briar. People all know me as Charles Shields's stuck-up daughter. If I want to be seen differently, I have to go somewhere else."

"You're the least stuck-up person I know."

She laughed but it wasn't filled with mirth. But hey, it was better than crying. "Trust me, my reputation as an awful person is well deserved."

He sat quietly for so long she doubted he was going to speak. She didn't know what else to say, so she was silent as well.

"You were angry at me at first, but I deserved it," Rick finally said. "But you've always been wonderful to Bobby. He adores you. And I—"

She cut him off before he could continue. She didn't want to know how he felt. Not yet. "I pretty much alienated everyone in town. I was the classic mean girl in high school. I tormented so many people just so I could feel better about myself. I targeted people who weren't in a position to fight back. I was horrible. I got worse when our engagement ended."

"You mean when I didn't show up to the church." His voice was filled with self-loathing.

"Yeah. My pride was hurt. I felt like everyone was laughing at me, thinking that I had finally gotten what I deserved. I'm sure some people did believe that. But everyone? Probably not. I believed it, so that was all that mattered. I put up walls and pushed people away, snubbing them before they could hurt me. The only thing I had left was my pride. And I used it like a shield. In my quest to make my father forgive me for what he perceived as my failure, I became more and more like him, taking on his worst qualities. As a result, I alienated everyone."

"Including your sisters."

"Yeah." She looked into his brown eyes. They were filled with such compassion she almost broke down. She looked away. "It's too late to change things in Sweet Briar, but I'll be able to start over somewhere else."

"I don't think that's true."

"Why? You think I'm so terrible that no one anywhere will ever like me?"

"That's not what I meant. I mean you don't have to move in order to start over. You can make plenty of friends here. All you have to do is let people see the real you."

"I'm not even sure who the real me is."

"I am. She's sweet and funny and sexy. Someone

kind enough to open her heart to a motherless young boy."

Her heart stuttered. Did he really think she was sweet? Sexy? "Bobby is easy to love."

"I talked to Carmen."

"You did? When?"

"Yesterday. She's willing to reconcile with you."

"She said that?" Her heart began to beat with joy. Could she really have her sister back?

"Yes. But she says you have to make the first move."

Her joy deflated. "Yeah, so she can slam the door in my face."

"I got the impression that's what you did to her."

"You'd be right."

"You two were always so close. What happened?"

Shame swamped her and she couldn't look him in the eyes. "She got in trouble when she was eighteen and my father put her out. I could have let her stay with me but I didn't. So she left town and didn't come back until our mother died. She tried to reconcile with us but our father was against it. I was still trying to gain his approval, so I kept turning her away. Finally she stopped trying."

"So call her."

She shook her head. "No. She's moved on. Her life is happy and uncomplicated. She doesn't need me or my mess."

"Call her," Rick repeated. "Or go to the youth center and see her. Whichever way is easier for you. Just reach out."

"She's pregnant. The last thing she needs now is drama."

"You're afraid."

"Maybe a little. But I'm also being considerate. I

don't want to upset her. Maybe I'll contact her after she gives birth."

"Okay. I don't agree with you, but I respect you and your opinion."

"Thanks."

He rose. "The charcoal should be about ready now. I'll put the food on the grill."

Half an hour later he called the boys to eat, reminding them to wash their hands first. Charlotte was putting condiments on the table when the boys came thundering onto the patio. If she didn't know better she would have sworn there were at least ten kids present instead of just two. Little boys definitely knew how to maximize noise.

"Hey, Charlotte. I didn't know you were here yet." Bobby's face lit with delight. His unconditional love chased away her gloom.

"I came the back way." She gave him a quick hug, which seemed to startle him as much as it shocked her. She'd never been the touchy-feely type. Since she had a snowman for a father it wasn't much of a surprise. She turned to Nathaniel, who seemed a little bit shy. "Hey. It's good to meet you. I've wanted to meet Bobby's best friend for a long time."

He smiled. "It's nice to meet you, too."

Rick placed a platter of hot dogs, burgers and grilled chicken in the center of the table. A minute later he added a bowl of potato salad, a mixed fruit salad and sliced vegetables. Everyone filled their plates. Charlotte noticed that each of the boys had placed baby carrots and sliced cucumbers on their plates without being prompted.

"They aren't so bad with dip," Bobby said, holding

out a carrot to her. A glob of ranch dressing dropped onto the table.

She glanced at Rick, who looked at her innocently. She couldn't leave Bobby hanging, so she took the offered vegetable and put it on her plate.

"Taste it," Bobby prompted.

Sighing, she picked it up between her two fingers and took a bite. It wasn't the worst thing she'd eaten in her life. She'd once found half a worm in an apple. She finished off the carrot and resisted the urge to follow it up with a can of pop. Instead, she forced a smile. "Not bad."

"You need to eat vegetables so you can be strong like us."

"Thanks for the information."

"You need more than one to be as strong as us," Rick mimicked, piling veggies on her plate and slathering them with dressing. She glared at him but he only winked and engaged the boys in a conversation about basketball. He was so going to pay for this.

Charlotte managed to choke down the vegetables without gagging. There was definitely a reward in her future. The box of cupcakes in her pantry would be just what the doctor ordered. Well, maybe not Dr. Tyler, the vegetable pusher, but Dr. Charlotte, lover of junk food.

After dinner, they washed the dishes then engaged the boys in a free-throw shooting contest. Charlotte won hands down. She would have thought they were letting her win if not for the surprised expressions on their faces. Charlotte was an excellent basketball player. She'd be a big asset to the women in the youth center's annual battle of the sexes basketball tournament. Of course, she hadn't been asked to join the team.

Nathaniel's uncle arrived a short while later with two little girls in tow. The girls tumbled out of the car and raced to Nathaniel, hugging him as if they hadn't seen him in years. He hugged them back, smiling. Clearly he wasn't the least bit embarrassed by their affection. She blinked back tears. She was turning into a big mushy mess.

Rick introduced Charlotte and Paul. She noticed Rick kept a proprietary hand on her waist. In light of their new friendship, she didn't embarrass him by moving away. Did he really think she would be open to starting a relationship with anyone when she was leaving town? Not that she was remotely interested in Paul.

The kids played with the ball for a few minutes before Paul hustled his nieces and nephew into the car. Bobby stood at the end of the driveway, waving until they had driven out of sight.

"Did you have a good time?" Rick asked, putting his arm over his son's shoulder.

"Yeah. I did. Thanks for letting Nathaniel come over."

"No problem. He's welcome to come over anytime."

Bobby nodded, but he seemed lost in thought. Rick picked up on that, too.

"What's up, son?"

"Nathaniel has two sisters. He says they bother him sometimes, but he likes having them around to play with. I think I would like a brother or sister."

"I'm not married. You know it takes a man and a woman to make a baby."

"I know that. But you could marry Charlotte and she could have a baby."

They both turned and looked at her as if expecting her to say something. No way was she wading into that conversation. She'd never been a chicken but right now turning tail seemed the best thing to do. She cleared her throat. "Thanks for dinner. See you later." Then she headed for the hills and the safety of her own home.

A half hour passed before she was able to get a grip on her emotions. Bobby was just a kid. He didn't know what he was talking about. To him it was all so simple. He wanted a sibling. Rick and Charlotte spent time together. He, himself, considered Charlotte to be a good friend. So why shouldn't they get married and give him a brother or sister? Why not indeed?

The idea was ludicrous. So why did her heart skip a beat at the thought? Especially since the last time she and Rick had planned to marry, it ended in disaster.

"Why did Charlotte leave like that?" Bobby asked.

Rick glanced into his son's worried eyes. Bobby had no way of knowing his question had probably dredged up painful memories for Charlotte.

Just forgiving him had been a monumental step. The last thing she'd ever consider was marrying him. If there was any doubt about that, her reaction had squashed it. She'd run away from them like she'd stumbled upon a toxic waste dump. She didn't move that fast when she was riding her bike. "Remember she said she had work to do today."

"You don't think she's mad at me, do you?"

"For what?"

"Saying she should marry you."

"No."

"Because I think it's a good idea. I want a brother and she doesn't have any kids. I don't think she has any family at all. If she marries you, we can be her family. That way she won't be all alone anymore."

"Actually, she has a family." Family that didn't care a bit about her.

"Really? I never see them."

"Yes." A crappy father and two sisters who weren't interested in her life or troubles. Still, they were her family. "But we're getting off track. Charlotte and I aren't getting married."

"Why not? You like her, don't you?"

"Yes."

"She likes you, too."

That was debatable. "It takes more than that."

"What?"

"Love. The people have to be in love."

"I know that."

"Good. Then you know why Charlotte and I can't get married."

"Sure you can. All you have to do is make her fall in love with you."

"And how do you propose I do that?"

Bobby crossed his arms across his narrow chest. "How am I supposed to know? I'm just a kid. Do you expect me to do everything? I asked her. Now you have to do the rest. You always tell me to make a plan and follow it so I don't get waylaid. Now that's what you should do." With that decree, Bobby picked up the basketball and began practicing his free throws. No doubt being smoked by a woman had increased his determination to get better.

Rick supposed he should be honest with Bobby and tell him that even if Rick was the last man on earth, Charlotte would never agree to marry him. Not again. And that was all right with him. Truth be told, Rick wasn't any more eager to get involved with someone than Charlotte was. His marriage to Sherry and subsequent divorce and heartbreak weren't something he wanted to repeat. He was content with his life and didn't see a reason to complicate it by adding a woman to the mix. Especially one he had a bad past with. No, it was best to leave well enough alone.

Chapter Eleven

Charlotte peered out her front window, watching as Rick's Mustang pulled out of the driveway. She'd been careful not to move the curtain, but she was sure he'd seen her. He'd paused and stared at her side of the duplex before he got into the car. She'd felt his stare down to her very soul. Of course, it was possible she was being paranoid. How could he know she was spying on him?

Nonsense. He couldn't see through walls. Or her covered windows. Her imagination was getting the best of her. But ever since Bobby suggested she marry Rick and the way her heart had leaped in response, she'd been avoiding them. She stepped away from the window in disgust. When had Charlotte Shields turned into a ninny who skulked behind window treatments? She was a bold and confident woman. She wouldn't allow an innocent comment to change that.

Determined to act like the woman she knew herself to be, she pulled open her drapes, letting in the morning sunlight. It was such a beautiful day, it would be a pity to waste it inside for fear of running into her neighbors. And though she was loath to admit it, she'd missed them. Bobby might be a rascal, but he was her kind of rascal. She wasn't much for children who bordered on perfection. There was nothing wrong with a kid who made messes and more noise than should be possible for one small person. In fact, she preferred that kind of kid.

Her house was too clean and too quiet. Too empty. She missed her afternoon snack with Bobby. The excuses she'd given him had been so lame she knew he hadn't believed them.

What if she'd hurt his feelings? That would be awful. He'd already suffered because of his mother. As soon as he got home from the youth center she'd invite him over for chocolate sundaes or banana splits.

Her phone rang and she answered without looking at the caller ID. Maybe it was one of the headhunters calling with a prospective job offer.

"Hello."

"It's Rick. I forgot today was Bobby's field trip to the beach. I'm at the youth center signing the permission slip, but he doesn't have his swim trunks and towel. I have a patient in ten minutes and don't have time to run home and get them. The kids are leaving in about half an hour. Would you mind bringing them to him?"

"Uh, sure. But how am I supposed to get in your house?"

"Through the garage. I installed a garage opener with a keypad." He gave her the code. "Thanks, Charlotte. I owe you."

She hung up the phone and hurried next door. After letting herself into Rick's house, she dashed into Bobby's room. Part of her was tempted to detour into the master bedroom, but she wouldn't. She could barely sleep without dreaming of Rick. The last thing she needed was to get a picture of his bed stuck in her mind, making it possible to imagine him there. And her with him.

She opened the drawer where she'd placed Bobby's swim trunks. Wonder of wonders, the swimsuit was where she'd put it. Of course, the rest of the room looked a little worse for wear. Bobby had confided that he made the bed while he was still in it, pulling the blankets up to his chin and then sliding out. It looked like it. A few toys were scattered around the room and his pajamas were balled up in a corner. She was pleased to see a book on his bedside table even if it was face down, damaging the spine.

Swim trunks in hand, she headed to the linen closet for a towel. In less than three minutes she was on her way to the youth center.

Two school buses were idling in the parking lot near the door, so she parked at the far end. She grabbed Bobby's suit and towel and hustled inside.

The area just past the reception desk was loud and chaotic. Kids were milling around with no apparent direction, laughing and talking while a few adults flipped through clipboards. The leaders could definitely use a lesson in organization. There was no way she'd allow anything she was in charge of to be so disjointed.

She took a closer look, which revealed what she hadn't seen the first time. The younger kids were grouped together by size and probably age, forming several crooked lines. The teens were clustered around the edges of the room. Then she saw Joni Danielson, who began ringing a bell. The voices gradually quieted until the room was silent.

Joni glanced at the now attentive kids. "Okay, everyone, we're going to start boarding the buses. Do you all have your suits and towels?"

Most of the kids nodded and a few held up cloth bags.

"I don't have mine," Bobby yelled. "My dad was going to get it and bring it to me."

"Okay. Hopefully he'll get here before the buses leave."

Charlotte was about to let Joni know she had the suit when Bobby spotted her.

"Charlotte!" He raced over, skidding to a stop an inch before he crashed into her. Smiling, she handed him his suit and towel. He squeezed her waist, somehow managing to squeeze her heart as well. She wrapped her arms around his skinny shoulders and hugged him back. Man, she loved this kid.

She looked up. Not only had the room become even quieter, but every eye was on them. She'd never minded being the center of attention before, but now unease made her skin crawl. She knew most people in town didn't like her and she could feel their animosity. In the past she'd chalked the dislike up to jealousy and considered it their loss. She was Charlotte Shields, daughter of the state's biggest employer. Now their antipathy hurt and she wished yet again that she could undo the past.

More than that, she didn't want the animosity people felt for her to flow onto Bobby. He had begun to make friends in Sweet Briar. Hopefully his association with her wouldn't make mothers tell their kids they couldn't hang out with him. He'd be crushed and he'd lost too much already.

She stepped back from Bobby. "Get in line. You don't want to be left behind."

Grinning from ear to ear, he ran back to his place beside Nathaniel, who waved at her. She waved back as discreetly as possible. The other women were staring at her, a couple with curiosity but most with open hostility. Okay, she got it. Nobody liked her. No reason to rub it in.

Affixing her public armor, she plastered on her political smile and focused her attention on Joni. "I'm sorry for interrupting. Dr. Tyler asked me to bring his son's suit. I'll be on my way so you can continue with what you were doing."

Charlotte began backing away.

"Charlotte," a soft voice said.

Charlotte turned. Carmen stood there. Though she held her chin high, there was a wariness in her eyes. Her heart pounding, Charlotte could only stare. Her sister was hugely pregnant. Before Charlotte had quit her job, she'd overheard several of the secretaries mention how nice it was that Carmen was expecting twins. A few months earlier, Charlotte and Carmen had come face-to-face. Charlotte had been with their father, so naturally she hadn't spoken. Self-loathing consumed her as she recalled the hurt on her sister's face. She'd let her need for approval from their mean-spirited father keep her from sharing in what had to be one of the happiest times of Carmen's life.

Shaking her head, Carmen took a step backward and Charlotte realized she hadn't said a word. No doubt her sister thought she was continuing to snub her. Reaching out, Charlotte touched her sister's hand before she could move away. "Carmen. It's so good to see you."

Carmen rolled her eyes and her lips turned down.

"It's true," Charlotte persisted. "I'm just surprised you'd even speak to me after how horribly I've treated you. You should hate me."

"You're the one filled with hate, Charlotte, not me."

Charlotte opened her mouth but couldn't think of anything to say. She certainly couldn't deny Carmen's words. The kids marched across the floor and she stepped aside to let them pass. Bobby smiled and waved one more time, his face lit with anticipation.

"That's Rick's kid, right?"

Charlotte smiled. "Yes. Bobby."

"The two of you seem close."

"He's a great kid."

"That's funny. They haven't lived in town a month and he seems quite attached to you."

Did Carmen have something against Bobby? She hoped not. She wanted a chance to restore her relationship with her sister, but not at the expense of the one she and Bobby were building. "What's your point?"

"Just that you seem so attached to Rick's child. Rick's the one who hurt you, embarrassed you in front of the entire town, yet you've let him back into your life. You and his son are close. I tried and tried to get you to forgive me for hurting our family and you shut me down every time."

Though Carmen spoke softly, Charlotte clearly heard the pain in her sister's voice. Carmen had idolized Charlotte when they were younger, yet Charlotte had let her need for her father's approval ruin their relationship. That nonsense was over. Starting now, she was going to be the sister she'd once been. Beginning with an apology. "I'm so sorry, Carmen."

It was as if her sister didn't hear her. "Of course, Daddy always liked Rick, so he must be pleased. He must approve if he let you leave work to bring Rick's son his swim trunks." Carmen's eyes swept over Charlotte and widened. "Wait. Why are you dressed like that on a workday? Where is your suit? And pumps? And makeup? What's going on?"

"Do you really want to know? If you do I would love to tell you. But first, I have to apologize for my behavior. I'm so ashamed. I don't deserve your forgiveness and I certainly don't deserve to be a part of your life. But I'm asking for whatever crumbs you're willing to toss in my direction."

Carmen didn't answer. Instead, she rubbed her back.

"Are you okay? Do you need to sit down? Of course you need to sit down."

"I'm fine but I wouldn't mind sitting down to continue this conversation. Do you have time?"

"I have nothing but time."

"Okay. Then let's go to the volunteers' lounge."

Charlotte followed her sister through the now empty youth center. Neither of them spoke until they were seated in comfortable chairs with bottles of water. Carmen looked directly into Charlotte's eyes. "So what's going on with you?"

"Well, for starters, I no longer work for Shields Manufacturing."

"What happened?"

Charlotte felt the sting of tears and she immediately blinked them away. Though she was determined not to shed another tear, her emotions were too strong to hold back. "I quit."

"You quit? But you love working there. That place is food and oxygen for you."

"I wish I could say you're wrong, but you're not. At least not entirely. I liked the work, but mostly I was trying to prove myself worthy."

"Of love?"

"Yes. How stupid is that?"

"Everyone wants to be loved. Especially by their parents."

"I finally figured out that it wasn't going to happen. He doesn't love me. Maybe he can't love me."

"How did you reach that conclusion?"

Charlotte noticed her sister didn't try to convince her

she was wrong. But then, Carmen had figured out long ago that their father didn't love any of his children. "He hired someone else to run the company. He gave the job I'd worked my entire life for to a complete stranger. He introduced him to the executive staff, myself included, at a special meeting. So I stood up and walked out."

"Good for you."

"It felt good."

"So now what?"

"I'm looking for a new job. I've had a few phone interviews with companies out of state. All of the jobs sound promising. And my headhunter has a couple of other interviews lined up."

"You're leaving Sweet Briar?"

"You did."

"I didn't have a choice."

"I'm so sorry. You have no idea how much I regret the way I acted back then."

"It hurt to have you and Charmaine turn away from me—I won't lie. But I survived. And now I am happier than I ever imagined I could be." She rubbed her hand over her enormous stomach, a dreamy look in her eyes.

"I'm so glad. You deserve to be happy."

"What about your relationship with Rick?"

"There is no relationship with Rick. He lives in the other side of my duplex."

"Really? How...awkward."

Charlotte laughed. "That's one word for it."

"What's another?"

Charlotte looked at her sister, amazed that they were talking so easily after all this time. She knew there was a long way to go before their relationship was close again, but it felt good to make a start. "Confusing. That man is so frustrating. When he got to town, he apologized every time he saw me. As if words could change the past."

Carmen grimaced. "Typical clueless male."

"Then there's Bobby. I don't know why, but that kid has taken a shine to me."

"You don't give yourself enough credit. You were great to me when I was his age."

"Until I stopped being great."

"That was a shock. But I understand now. You were caught between me and Daddy. There was no way I could win that one."

"Not then," Charlotte admitted.

"So what about Rick?"

"I don't know. I'm not angry at him now. I wish I could be, but there's something about him. I hate to admit it, but I'm still attracted to him."

"Maybe you guys have a second chance."

"No way. He burned me once. That's more than enough. Besides, I'm leaving town as soon as I get a job. I want to start over someplace where no one knows me. A new city where I don't have a horrible reputation."

"You can start over here. I did. My reputation was just as bad as yours."

"You were a bad kid. I was a bad adult. There's a difference."

"Not if we've both changed. And if you can start over in Sweet Briar, will you stay? And will you give a relationship with Rick a chance?"

Charlotte didn't answer. Would she willingly put her heart at risk for a chance to be with Rick? She didn't know, but she knew she had to figure it out soon.

Chapter Twelve

Rick stood on Charlotte's stoop, a box of candy in one hand and a bouquet of flowers in the other. He'd poured over fifty bite-size bars into a shoebox, which he then wrapped in thick red paper and tied with a silver bow. Most women preferred expensive candy, but Charlotte wasn't among them. He remembered like yesterday how she'd hit the grocery store on November 1 so she could grab up the Halloween leftovers at a 35 percent discount. She'd changed in many ways, but she hadn't lost her sweet tooth.

She answered the door, a smile on her face. She looked around him and her smile turned to a look of confusion. "Where's Bobby?"

"Still at the beach. There's a cookout followed by a movie. I don't have to pick him up until nine."

"Okay. Then why are you here?"

"I wanted to thank you for bringing Bobby's suit to

him." When she only stared at him, he lifted the box and flowers. "And I come with gifts."

"I'll take those." She opened the door and held out her hands.

"Really? You're going to take my presents and leave me standing out here all alone."

"You can always go home."

"That's cold."

She laughed. "Come in."

"Or you could come out."

"And do what?"

"Since I have a few free hours, I thought we could do something fun."

"I don't know."

"Come on, Charlotte. You know you want to."

"What did you have in mind?"

"I have a couple of steaks that I can put on the grill. I can add some potatoes and a salad."

"You had me at steak but lost me at salad."

"Vegetables are an important part of a healthy diet."

"Says who?"

"Me. I'm a doctor. I know these things."

"Actually, Doctor, fruit and vegetables are part of the same food group. I eat plenty of fruit so I'm covered."

"Okay. We'll have fruit salad."

"I'm in. Just give me a minute to put these in a vase." He stepped inside with her. "Take your time."

"I'm going to put these in my room. I'll be right back."

He watched as she jogged up the stairs, her round bottom attracting his eyes. After a moment, she skipped back down the stairs, a smile on her face. She looked absolutely stunning. Her shorts showed off her long shapely legs. Her blouse wasn't tight, but it emphasized her tiny waist and perfectly shaped breasts. She was so beautiful he couldn't look away.

She grabbed her keys. "I'm ready."

"Let's go."

He took her hand as they crossed the lawn. It felt so natural. So right. That thought stunned him and he nearly tripped up his front stairs. There was no way he was going to start thinking crazy things like that.

"I love steak," Charlotte said as he opened his front door and led her to the kitchen. She pulled out a chair, sat and crossed her legs.

"I remember." And he did. It amazed him just how many little things he remembered about her, especially given the amount of time that had passed since they'd last had any prolonged contact. Sure, he'd thought of her from time to time, but not in a romantic sense. He'd been absolutely faithful to his marriage vows. He'd simply wondered how she was getting along and hoped she was happy. Now his chest ached when he realized she wasn't. At least not as happy as she deserved to be.

"Would you like a drink?"

"Sure. What do you have?"

"Wine. Soda. Water."

"Wine sounds nice. Do you have red?"

"I do." He'd picked up a bottle on the way home. "Do you mind taking care of that?"

"Not at all." She looked at the label. "Nice. This is one of my favorites."

"I remember. Glasses are on the second shelf," he said, nodding toward the cabinet nearest him. She stepped closer and her delectable scent teased his nostrils and filled him with desire. The temptation to pull her into his arms nearly overwhelmed him. Where had that thought come from?

The perfume she wore was light and sweet. Or maybe the sweetness was simply her own personal scent. Whatever it was, it was driving him crazy. If he didn't move now, he was going to kiss her. He opened the door to the deck. "I'll get the charcoal going."

He'd managed to get his desire under control by the time the door opened behind him. Turning, he watched as Charlotte walked toward him, a wineglass in each hand. Her hips swayed seductively as she closed the distance between them. He accepted the wine when what he really needed was a gallon of water to douse the fire raging inside him. "Thanks."

She lifted the glass to her lips and his eyes followed. There was something so sexy about the way she sipped her wine. She sighed loudly. "I suppose I should offer to help you prepare dinner."

"Now, there is an offer I'll have to refuse, despite how graciously you extended it." He set his glass on the table near the grill. "If I didn't see both of your arms, I'd think one of them was twisted behind your back."

She laughed, and lust pure and simple roared to life. He'd been around Charlotte many times since he'd moved back to town. Although he'd noticed how beautiful she was, he hadn't been attracted. So why was he now? What had changed? And how did he change it back?

"I don't mind helping. What would you like me to do?"

"Actually, I have everything under control. The steaks are seasoned and the potatoes are scrubbed. All you need to do is sit down and relax."

"That I can handle."

He pulled out a chair and sat beside her, simply enjoying her company. One of the things he missed about being married was having another adult around to talk to. Not that he and Sherry had done a lot of talking in the months before she left. Or all that much in their marriage, come to think of it. He had Bobby, of course, but their conversations weren't the same. Nor should they be. Bobby needed to talk about his life and feelings, not listen to how his father often felt lonely for female companionship.

"Thanks again for bringing Bobby's suit to him. I appreciate it."

She waved a hand, brushing away his thanks. "No problem."

"Bobby's missed you these past few days. He was worried at first, thinking he'd done something wrong. Then I told him we probably scared you when he suggested you marry me. I told him you'd eventually come back around."

"I wasn't scared," she said, just as he'd expected. Her pride wouldn't let her admit to being afraid of anything.

"No? Then what were you?"

Charlotte tried to get her brain to function well enough for her to formulate a coherent answer to his question. An answer that didn't reveal her confusion.

He looked so relaxed. Nothing in the way he casually sipped his wine revealed his inner thoughts. Even so, she knew he had an idea of how his question affected her.

"Well," he prompted when she just sat there.

"I was a little…"

"A little?"

"Rattled, okay? Bobby's just a kid and doesn't understand what it means to talk about marriage. Especially when it comes to you and me, and our history. He just wants a woman in his life who loves him like his mother should have. I completely understand. I was shook up for a minute. I'm better now, but with our past, we shouldn't even joke about marriage."

"You're right. Which is why I brought it up. You and I are becoming friends, which is important to me. I don't want a misunderstanding to ruin that."

"Exactly. We tried the whole marriage thing. Or at least the engagement part. We never quite made it down the aisle." She tried, but didn't manage to keep the bitterness out of her voice. She was over the past, so she shouldn't still feel bitter. She shouldn't feel anything. But deep down she was still hurt and probably always would be.

"I'm sorry."

"I know. I shouldn't have brought it up."

"Maybe you haven't forgiven me."

"That's just it. I have. It must be all this crazy talk of marriage that's gotten me twisted up inside."

He touched her hand and electricity zinged through her. That wasn't good. "How about we put all this behind us and change the subject."

"Good idea."

He put the meat on the grill then placed a large bowl of mixed fruit in front of her. She speared a grape. "There is no way you just made this."

He chewed a chunk of melon. "No. I made it before I invited you to dinner."

"You were awfully sure of yourself."

"Not really. Bobby loves this stuff."

They leaned back in their chairs and watched the clouds float overhead. Amazingly enough, even after their earlier conversation, Charlotte felt at ease. After a while, Rick checked the temperature of the steaks and declared them ready. He placed them on plates along with potatoes and corn before joining Charlotte at the table.

As they ate, Rick entertained Charlotte with amusing stories from medical school and she laughed more than she had in years—or ever.

After she cleaned her plate, Charlotte leaned back in her chair and smiled. "That was delicious. Thanks for inviting me."

"You're quite welcome."

Charlotte looked up at the darkening sky. "It really is a beautiful night."

Moving his chair so near hers that she felt the heat from his body, he took her hand into his. "It's not nearly as beautiful as you are."

Her heart skipped a beat at his whispered words. "I thought we agreed to keep things strictly friendly."

"Maybe. But that doesn't mean I'm blind." His eyes met hers. She tried to look away but found herself held captive by his eyes. Oh, no, she was sinking into him again and she didn't think she would be able to get away this time. Worse, she wasn't sure she wanted to.

Chapter Thirteen

Rick's mind spun. What was he doing? He didn't have room in his life for romance. He could still smell the smoke from being burned by Sherry. But when Charlotte looked at him with her big brown eyes, her full lips slightly parted, he couldn't recall any of the reasons why kissing her was wrong. Leaning in, he brushed his lips across hers. Gently. Tentatively. When she sighed against his mouth, he wrapped his arms around her shoulders and kissed her again. This time more firmly. More deeply.

After a brief moment, she pulled away. "Your phone is ringing."

"What?"

She rose and disappeared into the kitchen, then emerged carrying his cell phone. He answered immediately, the fog of lust clearing from his mind as he listened.

"Is there an emergency?" Charlotte asked after he ended the call.

"Yes. Madelyn Nelson's baby has a fever and a rash. She and her husband are going to meet me at the office."

"Do you need help?"

"Not at the office. But I won't be able to pick up Bobby. Can you get him for me?"

"No problem."

He didn't like that a child was sick, but that phone call might have saved him from making a huge mistake. And getting involved with Charlotte would be a mistake. So why did kissing her—being with her— feel so right?

Charlotte waited until Rick had left before she dropped into a chair. What in the world had she been doing kissing Rick? True, he'd kissed her first, but after the shock wore off, she'd kissed him back enthusiastically.

And wow. What a kiss! Her lips were still smoldering from the heat of Rick's. She brushed her fingers across her mouth, trying to recapture the sensation.

Was she insane? This was Rick Tyler. The man who'd left her standing at the altar and then vanished from her life for a dozen years. She'd vowed not to let him anywhere near her heart. Yet somehow she'd ended up in his arms. There was no taking that back. And truly, it felt so good she didn't want to. But still, she couldn't repeat it. Rick's lips were officially off-limits.

She checked her watch. It was 8:40, time to pick up Bobby. She grabbed her keys and made the drive to the youth center.

When she got there, she found several women standing in the lobby of the youth center, talking and laughing quietly. One of the women looked up and saw her, then elbowed the woman beside her. A hush fell over the room as everyone turned and stared at her.

If even one of the women had smiled, she would have returned it. But not one did. Of course, she'd done her part to alienate them, so she couldn't expect them to make the first move. Many of them worked for Shields Manufacturing or had someone in their family who did. Charlotte had lorded it over them, talking down to them and treating them as if they were less than she was. Carmen had been welcoming, graciously accepting Charlotte's apology, so maybe these women would as well. Of course, Carmen was her sister and they'd once been close, something she couldn't say of these women.

She scanned their faces. To her shame, she didn't know many of their names. This wasn't going to be easy, but if she wanted to become a better person it was necessary.

Taking the bull by the horns, a cliché she hated, she strode across the room to the women waiting for their children. "Hello."

A couple of the women smirked and exchanged amused glances. She was contemplating walking away when one held out her hand. "I'm Tanya. I'm picking up my daughters Mia and Maya."

Relief flooded her as she shook the other woman's hand. "I'm Charlotte Shields. I'm here to pick up Bobby. He's the son of one of my friends."

"Bobby Tyler?"

"Yes."

"So, the doctor is good enough for you," said one of the other women, a sneer twisting her unexceptional face.

"Janet," Tanya chastised gently. "That's not nice."

"You're new here, so you don't know what Charlotte is like. We went to high school together. Charlotte made my life a living hell. And not just mine. A lot of kids were targets. She thought she was better than us since our parents worked for her father."

Janet glared at Charlotte and folded her arms over her imaginary breasts. Charlotte chided herself for being catty, even if only in her mind. She was supposed to be becoming a better person.

Charlotte sighed. "You're right. I did. And up until a couple of months ago I still thought that. There's no excuse for my behavior. I apologize."

Charlotte's words seemed to take some of the wind out of Janet's sails. She blinked as if baffled.

Charlotte looked at the other women. "I owe all of you an apology. Or at least most of you. I've been rude and condescending and incredibly unfriendly. I know words aren't much, but that's all I have. I'm sorry."

The women exchanged glances. Clearly they weren't going to accept her apology. But then, she hadn't forgiven Rick the first time he'd asked.

"My sister works for your father's company. She said he hired someone else to run it," one of the other women said.

Charlotte grimaced. "Yeah."

"We all thought you were going to take over one day."

"Join the club." Though she tried, Charlotte couldn't keep the pain from her voice.

Once again the women exchanged looks.

"Okay," one of the women said.

"Excuse me?" Charlotte said, unsure of what the woman was talking about.

"We accept your apology."

"That doesn't make us friends," another added. "But we don't have to be enemies, either."

Charlotte's eyes burned with unshed tears, which she quickly blinked away. "Thank you. I don't deserve forgiveness so easily, but I appreciate it."

"So is there something going on with the doctor?" Tanya asked with a grin.

Charlotte thought about the kiss, then dismissed it as a one-off. "No. Rick and I have known each other for years."

"Really?"

"Yes." Charlotte noticed that several of the other women were listening, so she included them in the conversation. "Perhaps you don't remember, but we were engaged once. He left me standing at the altar."

One of the other women gasped. "Are you serious?"

Charlotte frowned, but the pain she normally experienced was absent. "Unfortunately."

"When?"

"I heard something about it, but not all the facts."

"What a creep."

The women spoke over each other, but Charlotte made out most of their words. They weren't so hostile to her now. Nothing bonded women like commiserating over failed romances. "We were young, only twenty-two. To be fair, Rick wanted us to tell our families we weren't ready to get married, but I was too scared. My father wasn't a fan of the word *no*. He still isn't. Afterward I was embarrassed. I thought everyone was laughing at me. I kept people at a distance so I couldn't see the glee in their eyes. And so they couldn't see the pain in mine."

"I can imagine that hurt," Tanya said. "But you seem to be friends now."

"It was twelve years ago. I don't hold grudges for more than eleven years."

The other women laughed. Even Janet smiled.

"We're friends now," she added. "And I absolutely adore Bobby."

Tanya nodded. "My girls have mentioned him. They say he's really good at basketball."

"He should be. He practices nonstop."

"He also has some crazy notion about giving up vegetables for Lent next year. Now my girls want to do the same. I wish I knew where he got that idea."

Charlotte was saved from having to reply by the sound of bus engines. Minutes later the room erupted in noise as the kids began filing inside, some running while others straggled in, dragging towels behind them. When Bobby spotted her, his face lit up and he raced over.

"Hi, Charlotte. Are you here for me?"

"No one else. Your dad had an emergency and asked me to pick you up. You don't mind, do you?"

"No. I'm glad." He hugged her tight. "Are we going to my house or your house?"

"Whichever you want. Your dad gave me his keys so we can go there. Or we can go to my house."

"Your house," he answered without skipping a beat.

She nodded goodbye to the other women, then wrapped an arm around Bobby's narrow shoulders and steered him out the door.

"I had the best time," Bobby said as he fastened his seat belt. "Did you know there are fish in beach water? I didn't. One swam around me. Me and Nathaniel tried to catch it, but it was too slippery and kept getting away."

Several cars formed a line, so she had to wait a minute before she could pull into the street. "Nathaniel and I."

"Yeah. Me and Nathaniel."

She shook her head and decided to leave the grammar correction for another day. And for another person, namely his father. "What would you have done with it if you had caught it?"

"I don't know. Probably kept it for a pet. I don't have a tank yet, so I would have put it in the bathtub."

"Fish need to stay in water in order to live."

"I know that. I would put water in the tub." He paused, then laughed. "Oh, yeah. Now I get it. If we had put it on the sand to bring home later, it would have died."

"That's right."

"Then I guess it's good that we didn't catch it."

She nodded and signaled before turning down their street. "What else did you do?"

"A whole bunch of things. We had all kinds of races. My favorite was the sack race. That's where you're in a pillowcase and you have to hop to the finish line. That's really fun. Then we had three-legged races. It's hard to run with your leg tied to someone else's. Me and Nathaniel were partners and we came in second place. Then we had to do boy-and-girl teams. I didn't like that at all. This girl named Robyn was my partner. We fell a couple of times. And she kept complaining about how much sand was getting on her clothes. Who cares about that? She made me wait for her to brush it off before she would even try to run. We came in last place. Even the little kids beat us." His voice was filled with disgust.

"Some girls care about their clothes," Charlotte said as they went inside and dropped onto her couch. She didn't imagine he would be awake much longer. His eyelids were already beginning to droop. She slipped off her sandals and he toed off his gym shoes, not bothering to untie the shoestrings. He had enough sand on his socks to fill a sandbox but didn't seem to notice.

"They had a lot of food. Hot dogs and hamburgers.

Even some barbecue. And a whole lot of chips. And juice boxes. I love juice boxes. I had three of those. Dad only lets me drink one a day, so don't tell him how many I had, okay?"

"Your secret is safe with me."

"We watched a movie, too. I've never seen a movie at the beach before. It was so good. And we had popcorn. Some of the big kids played volleyball, but that's boring. I played tag and Mr. Freeze with a bunch of kids." He closed his eyes and they immediately popped open again. "They had this big fire. We got to sit around it and make s'mores. This guy had a guitar and taught us some funny songs. Then Miss Joni said it was time to leave. I wish we could have stayed longer."

He yawned and shut his eyes. This time they stayed closed. He leaned back and a minute later he was sound asleep. Charlotte removed his socks, put his grubby feet on the couch, helping him to stretch out so he wouldn't wake up with a crick in his neck, then grabbed a thin blanket from the linen closet and covered him. He tossed a few seconds until he was comfortable then was still, his breathing even.

She smiled as she looked at the little boy, watching him sleep. He was so dear. It was going to hurt like heck to leave him. But now that she and Rick were friends again, it would be possible for her to keep in touch with Bobby.

She peered out the window at the dark night. It was getting late. She hoped there was nothing seriously wrong with the baby. Although she didn't know Madelyn or her husband, Dean, very well, she could imagine how afraid they must be. She'd be out of her mind if Bobby was ill. And he wasn't even hers.

A couple of hours later, she was dozing in one of the

kitchen chairs when she heard knocking on her front door. She jerked and pain shot through her neck. These chairs definitely weren't meant for sleeping. Stretching her neck, she hurried to the door before the knocking awakened Bobby. She switched on the porch light, illuminating Rick. Stepping outside, she pressed a finger to her lips, shushing him before he could speak.

"Bobby's sleeping."

"I figured he would be. Why didn't you take him home so he could sleep in his own bed?"

"He wanted to come here." She glanced at Rick. He looked exhausted enough to sleep standing up. "If you want, you can leave him here for the night and head home to bed."

"I'm tired, but I'm too wired to fall asleep."

"Do you want to come in for a while? I have lemonade."

"That would be great. Thanks."

"Be quiet, though. Bobby's on the couch."

He laughed. "A marching band could come through here blowing horns and clashing cymbals and he wouldn't hear a thing. When he goes to sleep he's out for the count."

"You're kidding. I've been tiptoeing around here so I wouldn't disturb him."

"Of course you were," he said, smiling.

"How is the baby?" Charlotte asked when they were seated and sipping glasses of lemonade. They'd decided to sit on the patio with the back door open so they could hear Bobby in case he awoke. Actually, she'd insisted on leaving the door open.

"Fine. We got the fever down pretty quickly."

"So what took so long?"

He smiled ruefully. "Dean was so worried that in his rush to get to my office, he tripped down a flight of stairs. Not only did he twist his ankle, but he managed to bang his head. It was bleeding profusely, but then, head wounds tend to do that. Thank goodness he wasn't holding the baby when he fell.

"Anyway, Madelyn got them to my office. Dean wouldn't let me look at his head until after I treated the baby. I'm a father, so I understand putting your child first. Fortunately, the baby only has an ear infection. It took ten stitches to close Dean's wound. And of course he sprained his ankle pretty badly. Once I got him patched up, I had to sterilize the exam room."

"I'm glad they're fine."

"Me, too." He stretched his long legs in front of him. "Did Bobby have a good time tonight?"

"That's an understatement. I won't give you the details because I'm sure he'll want to tell you himself."

"You're probably right." He put his glass on the table and reached for her hand. "I would rather talk about us anyway."

"There's no us to talk about."

"Really? You're going to pretend like that kiss didn't happen?"

"I was going to try."

He met her eyes. "To be honest, I had planned on doing the same."

"Then it's agreed. The kiss never happened."

"I said I *was* going to do that. I changed my mind."

"Why? We shouldn't let a good plan go to waste."

He laughed and a shiver shimmied down her spine. "Because it's not a good idea. It's actually a rotten one. Whether or not we want to admit it, there's something going on between us."

"So we're attracted to each other. It'll pass."

"What's between us is more than physical."

Charlotte squirmed in her seat. Part of becoming a better person meant being honest. In this case, honesty meant baring her soul to the one person she knew could rip her heart to shreds. "So what if it is? That doesn't mean we have to act on it. Being friends is enough for me."

"Is it? Because no matter how hard I tried to convince myself otherwise, I'm not sure it's enough for me."

Her heart skipped at his words and their implications. She didn't know how to reply.

Maybe coming out here alone was a mistake. Her backyard was secluded. The scent of flowers filled the air and the moon and stars were shining brightly in the sky. The setting was perfect for seduction if one had seduction in mind. Maybe he did.

"I missed you." He stroked his fingers over the back of her hand, sending tingles up and down her spine. "While I was cleaning the exam room, all I could think of was getting back to you and taking up where we left off."

He dragged his fingers up her arm, leaving a trail of fire. She fought a moan that badly wanted to escape her lips. Finally his fingers reached her jaw and he caressed her face. As though it was the most natural thing in the world, she turned to his hand and brushed her lips across his palm. His skin smelled vaguely of sanitizers, but beneath it she smelled his familiar, masculine scent.

"Oh, Charlotte," he murmured mere seconds before his lips brushed against hers. After a moment, he deepened the kiss.

This must have been what heaven felt like. Hot desire coupled with warm security. She longed for more of his touch. More of his kiss. More of him.

Even with her eyes closed she saw stars. They were brighter and more luminous than the ones hanging in the sky. And not just bright white. They were brilliant colors—green, blue, purple, red. Every color of the rainbow.

A car door slammed, followed immediately by the sound of voices. The spell was broken and not a minute too soon. She was making a mistake following her feelings instead of her brain. There was no denying her attraction to Rick. And there was no denying that she was halfway in love with him. It wouldn't take much for her to fall the rest of the way.

And then what? That was the question she couldn't answer. Did she want to marry him? He'd talked about attraction, but nothing else. He hadn't mentioned love or made any promises. And if he did, did she trust him enough to believe him? He'd made promises before. She'd let her heart lead her down a dangerous road once. She intended to be much smarter this time.

Rick felt Charlotte's withdrawal, but didn't know why she'd pulled back. Sure, the sound of their neighbors reminded them they weren't alone. After all, they didn't want to be caught making out like a couple of teenagers. But she'd done more than walk inside the house, allegedly to check on Bobby. She'd put up a ten-foot solid brick wall. Although he wanted to know what changed, he knew tonight wasn't the time to ask.

Blowing out a breath, he stood and pushed his chair under the table. He didn't blame her for being cautious. Hadn't he concluded earlier that he didn't want to risk getting involved with anyone? So what happened to make him reconsider?

He didn't need to think long. It was her kiss. Something about the feel of her lips on his awakened feelings in him that he thought had died. Hoped had died.

But it turned out his heart could still care and no amount of caution or rational plans could change that. Not that he was in love with Charlotte and thinking about marriage. He wasn't crazy enough to take that leap again. But he didn't see anything wrong with spending time together. And if something more developed? He'd worry about it then.

He found Charlotte sitting in the living room, her eyes fastened on Bobby as he slept. A lamp provided a small circle of light around her, making her appear serene.

"I'd better get out of here. You sure it's okay for Bobby to spend the night?"

"Positive."

"Then I'll take you up on that. Just send him home whenever you want. I'll be up early."

"Sleep in. I'll feed him breakfast and keep him entertained."

When they reached the door he turned to her. "You really are something special, Charlotte Shields. I'm so glad to have you in my life."

Unable to resist, he kissed her briefly and stepped outside before he did something crazy like ask if he could spend the night, too.

Chapter Fourteen

Charlotte sipped the last of her coffee while the summer breeze cooled her skin. Birds twittered in the trees before diving to the ground in search of the unfortunate early worm. Other birds hopped along, choosing a more leisurely way to find their breakfast. The day was going to be a scorcher, so she wanted to get as much pleasure from the more comfortable early hours as possible. She'd watched the sun rise over the horizon, its glorious color brightening the sky. Nothing lifted her spirits like the promise of a new day.

Bobby would be waking soon. No doubt he'd be ravenous. She usually rode her bike before eating, but she'd make an exception for him. They could eat first and then ride to the beach and hang out since he'd had so much fun yesterday. That would give Rick more time to sleep. And it would give her more time to figure out what the heck was going on between them.

It had seemed so simple before. He'd been a jerk

who didn't care for anyone other than himself. He certainly deserved her anger. Now that she was getting to know him better she realized he wasn't the person he'd been twelve years ago. He'd matured and was actually a good man. Recognizing the changes in him left her vulnerable to his charms. Did she want to risk it? After all, there was no guarantee that things would work out any better the second time around. And she was leaving town soon. How would that affect them?

She stood and went into the house. She wasn't going to solve this now. Besides, it was time to get started on breakfast. Bobby had begun stirring a little while ago. She'd covered him several times last night, but the blanket kept ending up on the floor. She peeked into the living room. As expected, he'd kicked off the blanket again. Bobby stretched, opened his eyes, smiled and sat up.

"Hi, Charlotte. Did I spend the night?"

"You did indeed. It was late when your dad got back and we didn't want to wake you."

"Cool."

"I'm going to make breakfast. There's a new toothbrush for you in the bathroom."

"To use now?"

"Uh, yeah. When did you think?"

He shrugged and stood up. "After I eat. It seems like a waste to brush my teeth before I eat and then again after."

"Nice try. I'm not rationing toothpaste or water. But if it makes you feel better, tell yourself that one of these times is for last night. Okay?"

Grinning, he headed for the bathroom. He really was something. She picked up the blanket and took it into the laundry room to be washed later. It was filled with so much sand it would be a miracle if any was left on the beach.

"What would you like for breakfast?" she asked when he charged into the kitchen, a smear of toothpaste on his jaw.

"You mean like cooked food?"

She nodded. She couldn't cook dinner, but she had mastered breakfast.

"Great. Me and Dad usually just have cereal. Can I have pancakes?"

"Absolutely. Would you like bacon or sausage with that?"

"Sausage."

"Do you want eggs, too?"

"Do you know how to scramble them?"

"Of course." She gathered the ingredients for pancakes while she had him dig out the pans she would need to cook. "Do you want to help?"

"Can I?"

"Yes. You can do the eggs." She let him break the eggs. Then while his head was turned she spooned out the broken pieces of shell floating in the bowl, hid them in a paper towel, then handed him a whisk. A minute later he was beating the eggs with vigor.

"This is fun. I like cooking."

"It's definitely more fun when you have someone to cook with."

"I can come over every day. So can Dad. He likes pancakes."

"I'll keep that in mind."

She mixed the batter, then showed him how to sprinkle a few drops of water on the pan to make sure it was hot enough. He spooned in the batter and then hovered by the stove, clutching the spatula so he would be ready to flip the pancakes. The expression on his face was so intense. Although he and Rick weren't related genetically, Bobby had definitely acquired many of Rick's mannerisms.

Charlotte helped Bobby flip the first pancake, then allowed him to do the next two on his own. The look of pride on his face was priceless. He was so loving and eager. How could his mother just turn her back on him and walk away?

They were putting the food on the table when the doorbell rang.

"I'll get it," Bobby exclaimed as he dashed out of the kitchen, leaving her to follow at a more sedate pace.

She felt Rick's presence before she even saw him. There was an elemental shift in the atmosphere whenever he was around. The oxygen became thinner, making it difficult for her to breathe. His nearness caused her senses to go on high alert. The nerves in her body began to tingle and become more sensitive. She tried to fight her reaction, but she was powerless.

"Dad's here," Bobby said unnecessarily. He smiled brightly and she knew he was no longer angry at his dad. His anger hadn't been strong enough to overwhelm his love. It just took time to heal after what his mother had done to them both.

"So I see."

"I hear I'm in time for breakfast." Rick's smile sent those darn shivers down her spine and she felt herself smiling in return.

"It's not just Cheerios or Frosted Flakes, either," Bobby said. "We made pancakes. Come on before everything gets cold."

"Are you sure there's enough for me?" Rick glanced at Charlotte but Bobby answered.

"Yeah. We made a ton, didn't we, Charlotte?"

"At least that much. Come on."

She started to follow Bobby, but Rick grabbed her hand. His gentle touch, the warmth of his fingers, made her weak. She inhaled deeply in an attempt to steady herself. Instead, she got a whiff of his clean male scent, which turned her knees to rubber. What was she—sixteen?

"I didn't mean to intrude."

"You're not." At least not when it came to breakfast. But he was playing on the lawn of her heart, ignoring the no-trespassing sign. She didn't know if he was aware he was still holding her hand, but she was. Still, she couldn't make herself pull away. His touch felt too good. Too right.

"I got Dad a plate," Bobby said from his place at the table. He'd already served himself, leaving a trail of scrambled eggs from the platter to his plate. He'd soaked his pancakes with syrup, which puddled around his sausage links. He didn't seem to notice. "And I poured us all some juice."

He certainly had. None of the three cups were more than three-quarters full, but there was an orange ring on the table circling each one. She wouldn't even try to figure out how that had happened. It was just as easy to wipe it up, which she did. Happily there was no juice on the floor, at least none she could see. "Thank you. You are a wonderful young man."

He beamed at her praise then dug into his breakfast. Charlotte grabbed a bowl of mixed fruit and a couple of containers of yogurt and set them on the table. She gestured for Rick to take a seat, but he didn't. Instead, he walked around the table and pulled out her chair for her. Murmuring her thanks, she sat, immeasurably pleased by his thoughtfulness.

She and Rick fixed their plates and began to eat. Rick sampled everything. "This is really good."

"I cooked the eggs and flipped the pancakes," Bobby bragged.

"Really? Maybe you should cook breakfast every morning so we don't have to eat cereal."

"I can't do it by myself. Charlotte has to help." Bobby looked from his father to her. "You should sleep over at our house tonight so we can make breakfast tomorrow."

Charlotte's fork dropped from her hand and clattered onto her plate, splattering syrup onto her top. Although she tried not to, her eyes lifted to Rick's face. He wiggled his eyebrows suggestively and grinned slowly. "I think that's a great idea, Bobby, but Charlotte might not like cooking for us two days in a row."

"Don't you want to cook for us?" Bobby looked disappointed at the thought.

Charlotte kicked Rick under the table and smirked when he jumped. "I do like cooking for you, but I don't usually eat this much for breakfast. But if you want, we can ride together some mornings."

"Okay. But you can still sleep over if you want, right, Dad?"

"She sure can. Our house is her house." He leaned in closer and for some inexplicable reason she did as well. Then he whispered so Bobby couldn't hear. "You're welcome to spend the night anytime you want."

She laughed. "In your dreams."

"Every night and even some days."

She shook her head. He was such a flirt. What would he say if he knew he'd been starring in her dreams since they'd kissed? He'd probably puff up like a peacock and strut around for the rest of the day. Or worse, he'd make some comment about making their dreams come true.

And since she didn't trust herself to refuse that offer, it was best to keep that information to herself.

"Really? They must not be pleasant dreams if you're up this early. I thought you were going to sleep in."

"I tried. My internal alarm clock wouldn't let me. Besides, why waste time dreaming of you when I can have the real thing just by coming next door? You're better than any dream. You always have been."

Rick watched Charlotte's eyes fill with tears and wondered what he'd said wrong. He was being honest. She needed to know how he felt about her. He replayed his words in his mind. Perhaps he shouldn't have mentioned the past. Maybe that reminder had her doubting his sincerity. He was just about to assure her when her lips trembled in a wavering smile.

"Thank you. That is the nicest thing anyone has ever said to me."

He gave her hand a gentle squeeze. Her skin was so soft. He was coming to believe her heart was even softer. "I meant every word. You are special."

"Hey, what are we going to do now?" Bobby asked. "Are we going to ride our bikes?"

Rick smiled at his son's eager expression even as he cursed his lousy timing. "You need to take a shower, young man."

"But why, Dad, if I'm only going to get dirty again? It's like a waste of soap and water. And you always tell me not to waste stuff."

Rick looked at Charlotte, who only shrugged. Clearly he was on his own. He could insist, but he didn't want to get into a long-drawn-out battle. *Compromise* wasn't a dirty word. "Well, you have to wash up and change your clothes."

"I can do that." Bobby hopped up, grabbed his plate and cup, and put them in the sink. "Then can we go riding? Can we ride to Nathaniel's house? I know where he lives. Maybe he can come with us."

"We'll see." Rick helped Charlotte clear the table and then followed Bobby into the living room. He wanted to take Charlotte's hand again but couldn't think of a smooth way to do so.

Bobby grabbed his balled-up towel and swim trunks. Something clattered to the floor. "Oh, yeah. I almost forgot about this."

"About what?" Rick asked.

"A shell. Nathaniel's little sisters wanted to give shells to their mom, so we helped them find some. There are a whole lot of shells on the beach. Miss Joni said if you put them up to your ear you can hear the ocean. But that's kind of dumb if you're *at* the ocean. You can already hear it. Anyhow, we found a whole bunch for their mom. And I got this one for Charlotte." Bobby stood and walked over to Charlotte. He opened his hand and offered the shell to her, his heart in his eyes.

"Thanks." Her eyes glistened and she blinked rapidly.

"This was the best one of all. And the biggest. There were two big ones, so they gave one to their mom and I took the other one for you." He looked up at Charlotte, his smile hopeful. "Do you like it?"

"I love it." She kissed his syrupy cheek. "This is the best gift I've ever gotten. Thank you."

Bobby grinned. "You're welcome. I can get you some more the next time I go to the beach. Then you'll have a whole bunch like Nathaniel's mom."

"I would love that." Charlotte clutched the shell to

her chest like it was a precious diamond. "But in the meantime I'm going to put this one someplace special."

Bobby looked around the room, considering and dismissing every surface. "I put all my special stuff in my room. It's in a shoebox under my bed. That way if someone breaks in our house they won't find it."

"I think my bedroom is a good place to keep it. I'll put it on the table by my bed so it will be the first thing I see every morning when I wake up and the last thing I see at night before I go to sleep. And every time I look at it I'll think of you."

Rick looked on as Charlotte and Bobby hugged each other. A strange warmth grew in his chest. The love Bobby and Charlotte felt for each other was obvious.

Bobby was the most important person in his life. Rick's concern for his son's feelings was the primary reason he'd been reluctant to get involved with a woman. He didn't want Bobby to feel like he had to compete for his attention. His son's easy acceptance of Charlotte removed that impediment. Of course, Rick still had to decide whether he was willing to take a chance on a relationship. That he didn't reject the idea outright was proof that he was falling for Charlotte. Surprisingly, he didn't mind.

Chapter Fifteen

"Charlotte really liked my gift," Bobby said as they crossed the strip of grass separating the two properties. When Charlotte realized Bobby was going to become not only a regular visitor, but one who didn't give a hoot about walking on the sidewalk, she'd placed stepping stones, preventing an unsightly dirt path from being worn in the lawn. Rick should have thought of it, but he hadn't.

"So can we ride bikes with Charlotte?" Bobby asked, not at all concerned that Rick hadn't replied to his previous statement. But then, Bobby was focused on his plan.

"Sure."

"Okay. I'll call Nathaniel and tell him we're coming over. I know he'll want to ride with us."

"Hold up. We need to ask his mom or his uncle if it's okay. They might have other plans."

"Okay. But I bet they won't mind."

While Bobby got cleaned up—he decided to take a shower after all—Rick called Nathaniel's uncle and received permission to take the boy bike riding. Paul actually seemed relieved. No doubt caring for his sick sister-in-law and her three children was exhausting. After ending the call, Rick went over to Charlotte's.

Her garage door was open, so he stepped inside. She was lowering her bike from the rack and once more he was struck by her beauty. Her body was strong and powerful, which, given her personality, suited her to a T.

As if she felt him checking her out, she turned. "What are you doing here?"

She'd changed into a tight cropped shirt that emphasized her perky breasts and revealed her incredible stomach. Her smooth skin covered toned muscles and a tiny waist. His mouth went dry and he couldn't speak to save his life.

"Well?" she prompted.

He said the first thing that came to his mind. "I'm just letting you know Bobby decided to take a shower after all."

"That's good. I didn't want to say anything, but he was this side of really ripe." She grabbed her helmet and placed it on her head, covering up her glorious mane.

"It's going to take us a couple of minutes to be ready, so you might want to take that off."

"Ready for what?"

"To go riding." He gestured to her bicycle. "Isn't that what you're getting ready for? To go over to Nathaniel's? Bobby mentioned it at breakfast."

"I never said I would come."

"You never said you wouldn't. He expects you to go with us."

She huffed out a sigh and leaned against her bike. "I

really need to get my exercise in today, especially after the breakfast I just ate."

"Your body is more than perfect and you know it."

"I don't know any such thing. And thank you."

"We'll be riding our bikes. That counts."

"You do realize that riding with you guys is not exactly strenuous exercise."

"Well, if you don't want to go, you're going to have to be the one to tell Bobby. I'm not going to be the bad guy."

"You don't want to go with us?" Bobby asked. He must have taken the fastest shower of his life. He'd changed into a pair of blue basketball shorts and a Chicago Cubs T-shirt. Although he loved playing basketball, he'd gotten swept up in Cubs fever when they were still living up north. He'd preferred them to the hometown Milwaukee Brewers.

"It's not that I don't want to come. I just really need a long and fast ride."

"Me and Nathaniel are fast and Dad won't get mad if we leave him behind. Will you?"

"I think I'll be able to keep up with you guys," Rick said dryly.

"Okay. Let's get our bikes. We'll be right back."

Charlotte sighed and Rick bit back a smile. He could practically see her brain spinning as she tried to figure out just how she had lost control of the situation.

Fifteen minutes later they pulled into Nathaniel's driveway. As they climbed off their bikes the front door opened and Nathaniel's uncle came outside. He smiled and greeted them.

"Is Nathaniel ready?" Bobby asked.

"Almost." Paul included Rick and Charlotte in his reply. "He's cleaning his room."

"You're like that, too?" Bobby asked in horror. "I thought only my dad made me clean up before I could have fun."

Paul shook his head. "It's all of us, uncles included. Let's go inside. Roz wants to meet all of you."

They went inside to the living room. A thin woman was sitting in a recliner that had seen better days. A crocheted shawl was draped over her shoulders and another covered her lower body. One of the side effects of cancer treatment was feeling cold. Rick examined her as subtly as he could. She wasn't his patient, but he was the only doctor in town. If she needed emergency treatment, more than likely he would be the one to provide it.

She smiled when they came in. Although her skin was dull, her eyes were bright and her smile was welcoming. "Hello. I'm Roz Martin."

Charlotte crossed the room and took the woman's hand into hers. Even from where Rick stood he could see how gentle she was as she introduced herself and took a seat on the couch. He followed suit, sitting beside Charlotte.

"Thanks for taking Nathaniel with you. Paul gave him a bike a few weeks ago and he's been dying to go on a real bike ride."

"It's our pleasure," Charlotte said. "Bobby talks about Nathaniel nonstop. He's his best friend in the whole wide world."

"Nathaniel feels the same way about Bobby. I wish I had the strength to go with you."

"How are you feeling?" Rick asked, taking the opening. "You may not know but I'm the new doctor in town. Is there anything I can do for you?"

"I'm actually having a good day. And yes, I know you're the doctor. It's good to have one nearby."

"Call me day or night if you need me."

"Thanks."

"Or me," Charlotte added. "I'm between jobs now, so if you ever need someone to run errands or just want to hang out, I'm available."

"That sounds like fun. I haven't spent time with another female in the longest time. At least not one over three feet tall."

"I don't want to impose, but if you feel like having company now, I can let Rick and the boys ride by themselves."

Roz smiled. "That sounds like bliss but I don't want to ruin your day out."

"You're not."

Rick watched Charlotte in astonishment although he shouldn't have been surprised. Charlotte was a kind person who recognized someone in need of a friend. Heck, she needed friends herself.

The boys raced into the room and Nathaniel approached his mother. "Uncle Paul says my room is clean enough so I can go. Will you be okay without me, Mom?"

Roz swallowed. "I'll be fine. You have a great time with your friend. Okay?"

"Okay." He kissed her cheek. "See you later."

Bobby followed his friend to the door then looked back. "Come on, Charlotte."

"I'm going to hang out with Bobby's mom. But you have fun."

He ran back, kissed her cheek and raced from the room.

"You aren't at all like your reputation," Roz said twenty minutes later. Once Rick and the boys had ridden away, Paul had brought Roz and Charlotte cold drinks, then left to help the girls clean their room. Charlotte figured it was his way of giving the women time alone.

"Have we met? I'm sorry I don't remember you."

Roz laughed. "You didn't do anything to me exactly. You just sort of ignored me, looking through me like I was nothing important. Dirt under your feet."

Charlotte grimaced. "I'm sorry."

"You don't need to apologize. If I hadn't listened to what other people had told me about you, I wouldn't have given it a second thought. Besides, I don't have the time or energy to hold grudges."

Charlotte's heart broke at the other woman's words. Roz truly was fighting for her life. "I'm sorry."

"The doctors are optimistic. I'm scheduled for surgery in a few weeks. Then another few rounds of chemo. After that I should be better."

Charlotte wasn't sure if Roz was being overly optimistic or if her prognosis was as good as she was saying. But if Roz was fooling herself, she was entitled. Charlotte certainly wasn't going to bring her down. "That sounds wonderful. When you're up to it I'll take you out to lunch to celebrate."

"I'd like that."

They were quiet for a few minutes. "You must be so relieved to have your brother-in-law here to help you."

"He's good with the kids and always polite to me."

Charlotte told herself to let the comment pass but she couldn't. It was such an odd choice of words. "Polite?"

"Paul and I have a past. Things didn't work out and I married his half brother."

"Ah. That can make things awkward."

"You don't know the half of it."

Charlotte raised a hand. "I'm practically a stranger

and it's not my business. Please don't feel compelled to tell me more than you feel comfortable sharing."

"I'm just grateful he showed up when I needed him. I'm not looking for anything more."

Charlotte nodded, not quite believing the other woman. She recognized the longing to be loved by a special man from her past. Perhaps because Charlotte had the same desire.

"You must think our relationship is odd."

"Not really. Rick left me standing at the altar twelve years ago. I didn't think I would ever forgive him, but now we're friends."

Roz laughed. "Okay, so I'm not alone. But tell me, do you trust him enough to start over with him?"

"I'm not sure." Charlotte wished she could say yes but she couldn't. What would it take for her to truly open her heart to Rick? She wasn't even sure she wanted to. And did he want a second chance? A couple of kisses didn't make a relationship. Maybe he was happy with the way things were. And if he wanted more, would she be open to it? She hated her doubts, but she didn't know how to get rid of them. Maybe she couldn't.

Roz lifted her glass of orange juice in a toast. "Here's to perplexing relationships and the men who confuse us to no end."

Charlotte tipped her glass and laughed. "I'll drink to that."

"You need to sign my permission slip," Bobby said, shoveling his spoon into his cereal. "Miss Joni needs them today."

"Permission slip for what?"

"For the sleepover at the youth center tomorrow night. Everybody's going. We're going to swim and play ball and a whole bunch of games. We get to stay for breakfast in the morning. Some of the kids went last year and they said it's a lot of fun."

"Sure. Give me the paper and I'll sign."

Rick read the permission slip and quickly scrawled his signature on the appropriate line. Bobby chattered excitedly as they finished eating and got ready to leave. Rick dropped Bobby at the center then headed to his office, his mind whirling. He was finally going to have a night to himself. There were a lot of things he could do around the house, but he'd rather have fun.

When he reached his office, he grabbed his phone. There was no one he'd rather spend time with than Charlotte. Hopefully she felt the same.

"What are you doing tomorrow?" he asked as soon as she answered the phone. His first patient wasn't due for another fifteen minutes, so he had time to talk.

"Hello to you, too."

"Hi. So, do you have plans for tomorrow night?"

"No. Why?"

"Bobby's spending the night at the youth center. I thought we could have a night on the town."

"In Sweet Briar? The town might have grown, but the streets still roll up at ten o'clock."

"Nothing says we have to stay here. We can go to Willow Creek. Or even farther."

"I don't know, Rick."

"What's not to know?"

"What we're doing. I, for one, don't have a clue."

"Don't overthink things. We're just two friends who enjoy each other's company and who're both free tomorrow and decided to do something together."

"Is that all?" Charlotte sounded suspicious.

All that he was willing to admit to. "Yep. So are you in?"

"Willow Creek has several places to choose from. And it would be nice to go out." She hesitated and he held his breath. "Okay. I'm in."

"Great. I'll call you later and we can firm up the details." Rick hung up and grinned. He was looking forward to tomorrow night just as much as his son was.

Charlotte looked at the pile of clothes on her bed and shook her head. She was acting like a fifteen-year-old going on her first date with a gangly, pimply-faced boy. But she was a grown woman who'd been on dates before. Still, she wondered if her aqua jersey cocktail dress was the right choice. With beads scattered around the plunging neckline, it was a bit on the slinky side. But she loved the way it clung to her body, showing off the figure she worked hard to maintain. Rick had been pretty vague on the details, only saying she should dress for a good time. What the heck did that mean? Perhaps she should swap this dress for her red silk. Or her black wrap dress. You could never go wrong with black.

She stepped away from the full-length mirror. She was not changing clothes a fifth time. If he wasn't happy with the way she looked that was too darn bad. Snagging her purse, she glanced at the shell Bobby had given her and, as always, she smiled.

Her doorbell rang precisely at seven o'clock as she knew it would. She didn't delude herself into thinking Rick was anxious to see her. He'd always been prompt, believing it was disrespectful to be late.

Telling her rapidly beating heart to calm down, she crossed the room, opened the front door and bit back a gasp. Rick was good-looking when he was dressed in jeans and shirts. He was heart-stoppingly gorgeous in a gray suit and white shirt. He smiled and she hoped her heart would stay in her chest.

"Wow. You are positively stunning," Rick said as he stepped forward, closing the distance between them. He wrapped an arm around her waist and gave her a quick hug. "You smell good, too."

She gave up trying to control her heart. She'd follow its lead and see where she ended up. Hopefully she would find happiness this time. "Thanks. So do you. Do you want a drink?"

He shook his head. "No. Actually, I'd like to get this date started."

"You were pretty mysterious about your plans. Now can you share them with me?"

"I wasn't trying to be secretive. I thought we could go to dinner and talk. We haven't had much time alone. Then I thought we could go bowling. I remember how much you always liked it."

Bowling had been an immense pleasure of hers. Growing up, she'd spent nearly every free moment at the bowling alley. It was a sport that didn't require a friend. "Sweet Briar Lanes closed years ago."

"I know. There's a bowling alley in Willow Creek. They have candlelight bowling on Fridays. I already booked us a lane."

"Great. I'll go grab a change of clothes."

She hurried from the room. Tonight was going to be the best night in forever.

Chapter Sixteen

"Strike!" Charlotte spun around with her hands over her head and shimmied her hips in celebration.

"Are you sure you haven't bowled in years?"

"Twelve, to be exact."

"Really?" He'd bent to pick up his ball from the return rack, but he straightened. "Why? You loved bowling. And you were good at it."

She nibbled on her bottom lip, trying to decide how much to tell him. Heck, she might as well be completely honest. "You and I had gone bowling so often. Once we ended things, it wasn't fun anymore. It reminded me of you and made my heart ache."

His eyes filled with shame and sorrow, which was not her intention. "Charlotte."

She waved her hand at him, shutting him up before he could apologize again. The past was over. "It's your turn."

He rolled his ball and watched as it knocked down

all ten pins. Strike. "Unlike you, I have been bowling. So this should be a good game."

She smiled. "I wouldn't be so sure of that. I think my first time must have been luck."

Sure enough, she rolled her next two balls into the gutter.

Rick laughed. "Looks like you're going to end up with a score of ten."

He picked up his ball and started his motion. Suddenly filled with mischief, Charlotte stepped next to him and blew in his ear. The ball flew from his hand and bounced into the gutter. She grinned and clapped. "Looks like you're going to have a ten, too."

"Playing dirty, are you, Miss Shields?"

She batted her eyelashes, something she'd never done in her entire life. She'd never flirted before, either. It was fun. So much fun she decided to do it again. "I don't know what you're talking about, Dr. Tyler," she said, walking her fingers up his firm chest. "You looked hot to me and I thought I would help you cool off."

A look of devilment on his face, he grabbed her wrist and pressed her hand against his chest. She could feel his heart thudding beneath her palm. "Blowing in my ear gets me hot. Very hot." He leaned down until his lips were only a centimeter away from hers. "So what do you intend to do about that?"

She closed that slight distance, touching her lips to his as she spoke. "I'm not sure what you're asking. Do you want me to cool you off or get you hotter?"

He pressed his lips onto hers in a brief but intoxicating kiss. Her knees wobbled and she felt giddy as a lovestruck teenager. She could kiss him all night. Except for the fact that they were standing in the middle of a twenty-eight-lane bowling alley that was currently filled with people, some of whom were staring at them. A man wolf-whistled and Charlotte reluctantly pulled away.

Rick wiped a hand across his forehead. "I think you just got me hotter."

She grinned wickedly. She was close to melting herself, but she wasn't going to share that bit of information. "It's still your turn."

"Maybe you should sit down first."

"Don't you trust me?"

"You smell like heaven and taste like something I can only dream of. It's me I don't trust." He pointed to their booth. "Sit."

"Okay." She kissed his chin, smiling when he inhaled a ragged breath. She put a little extra swing into her step as she swayed toward the bench. The hard plastic seat definitely wasn't meant for comfort, but it did provide an unobstructed view of Rick's perfect backside.

He knocked over all ten pins, giving him a spare. Grinning, he turned around. "Your turn."

"You need to sit down first."

He brushed a finger down her cheek, running the tip of his finger around her lips. Although she longed to lean into his touch, she forced herself to back away.

She took a few short steps, tossed the ball and watched as it knocked over two pins. At this point she didn't really care how many pins she knocked down or if she rolled gutter balls for the rest of the game. She just wanted more of Rick. More touches. More kisses. More everything.

Her ball returned and she grabbed it. This time she knocked down seven pins. "Your turn."

As she passed by, Rick grabbed her wrist. "Password."

"What?"

"You have to tell me the password if you want to sit down."

Playing along, she fluttered her eyelashes. "And if I don't know the password?"

One side of his mouth lifted in a sexy grin. "Then you'll have to pay the toll."

"But my purse is over there."

"You don't need money. It's not that kind of toll."

"I see." She leaned in closer, touching her breasts to his muscular chest. "What do you want?"

"Your body. But I'll settle for a kiss."

"Lucky for you I have one of those."

"One might not be enough, but given the fact that we're in public, I'll settle for that. For now."

"And later?"

"That depends on you. No pressure."

Her heart kicked up a notch in anticipation. Their flirting had definitely taken a turn for the serious. But then, the entire night could be considered foreplay. The evening had started with a candlelit dinner of simple yet delicious Italian food: lasagna for her and linguine in clam sauce for him, accompanied by a bottle of Chianti. They'd lingered over dessert of zabaglione and berries, feeding each other the sweet custard and raspberries. Then they'd held hands and taken a moonlit stroll through downtown Willow Creek.

Now they were giving gentle touches each time they passed. A small fire was smoldering in her stomach. Soon it would be an inferno that no amount of self-control could contain. Not that she wanted to.

She kissed him gently, teasingly, then sat down. Rick took his turn, rolling the ball down the lane in a most distracted manner. Then she took her turn, her manner much the same. Luckily, the system automatically kept score. She didn't think she could concentrate well enough to add properly. Not that either of them cared who won. They were more interested in touching and kissing.

Finally they reached the tenth frame. After rolling two gutter balls, she turned and smiled at him. "That's it for me. Looks like I bowled a sixty-two."

He took his turn then checked his final score and grimaced. "One hundred twenty-seven."

"Want to play again?" she teased. "How about two out of three?"

"Sure. Or maybe three out of five."

She laughed. He wasn't any more interested in bowling another game than she was. "Or maybe four out of seven. I want to give you a chance to redeem yourself by getting a higher score."

"I'm not interested in scoring. At least not here."

"In that case, let's return these shoes and get out of here."

They didn't talk much on the way home. Instead, they listened to a smooth-jazz station on the radio, letting the seductive sounds of the saxophone set the mood.

"My place or yours?" Rick asked as he pulled into the driveway.

She pictured the pile of clothes on her bed, the shoes and purses scattered around the room. Definitely not romantic. "Yours."

They held hands as they crossed the driveway, their stride unhurried in total contrast to the rapid beat of her heart. Each of her nerve endings was jangling and she was more aware of even the tiniest things. The rough callus on his palm brushing against her softer skin. The faint scent of his aftershave wafting into her nostrils when he leaned down to whisper into her ear. The heat emanating from his body that wrapped around her, making her stomach do a crazy loop.

He unlocked the door and let her step inside, keeping his hand on her waist as if he didn't want her to get too far from him. He needn't have worried. Right by his side was where she wanted to be now. Maybe for always.

Not that she would fool herself into thinking he was offering forever. Tonight was about tonight. And she was good with that. She didn't know where she'd be living in a few months, so she didn't have the future to offer. But tonight…tonight she was going to give everything she had.

He drew her into his arms and kissed her. Because of the lack of privacy, the kisses they'd shared at the bowling alley had been chaste. This kiss was nothing like those. It was hot and demanding, a knee-weakening affair. As she began sinking to the floor, he gripped her waist and swung her into his arms.

"I've waited all night for this," he murmured against her lips as he maneuvered through the first floor and up the stairs.

"A lifetime," she whispered, speaking the words that had been hidden in her soul. But this wasn't the time for keeping secrets. Now was the time for sharing even if that meant making herself vulnerable.

He shouldered the door open, then crossed his bedroom in three easy strides. He set her on his bed and stared deeply into her eyes. "Are you sure?"

She nodded. "More sure than I've ever been about anything in my life."

"I was hoping you'd say that." He began placing little kisses along the side of her neck, sending shivers down her spine that reached the tips of her toes.

"I was hoping you'd do that."

Easing down the zipper on her top, he brushed his lips over her shoulder. "I'm going to do a whole lot more."

"Promises, promises," she whispered as she unbuttoned his shirt and tugged it from his pants.

"A promise I intend to keep," he murmured before pulling her shirt over her head. After that they were silent for a long, long time. Words weren't necessary as they let their bodies do the talking for them.

Rick caressed the smooth and slightly damp skin on Charlotte's shoulder, brushing aside her soft hair. He loved the feel of the springy strands between his fingers. She'd snuggled up to him and fallen asleep about half an hour ago. He was sleepy himself, but he didn't want to miss one minute of holding her in his arms, breathing in her delicate scent.

The more time they were together, the closer he felt to her. She filled him with such incredible joy. When he was with her, it was as if his world was finally spinning properly. He hadn't been aware of how dull his life was until she'd brought color to it.

He was falling in love with her. One minute he'd been living his life, getting by the best way he could. The next he was realizing just how important Charlotte had become to him. How interwoven their lives had become.

He closed his eyes and searched his feelings. The discovery of his new emotions didn't bother him. In fact, he liked the idea of making Charlotte a permanent part of his life. After tonight, he believed she felt the same.

Chapter Seventeen

The feel of fingers caressing her skin, traveling up and down her back, gradually went from being a part of Charlotte's dream to a part of her reality. Sighing, she opened her eyes and found herself staring directly into Rick's. His lips were close enough to touch, so she did, dragging the tips of her finger around first the bottom lip and then the upper one. He smiled before he captured her finger and kissed it.

"Good morning, beautiful lady."

She ran a hand through her hair. "I doubt *beautiful* describes the way I look."

"You'd be wrong." He kissed her briefly. "I wish I had time to show you just how wrong you are."

"What time is it?" The sun was streaming through the window, so she knew she'd slept later than usual.

"Almost nine."

She sat up, pulling the blanket with her and covering her breasts. "Really? I never sleep this late."

"I know. Most days you're up before the sun. But then, you don't spend most nights making love over and over until you collapse."

She grinned. "Who told you that?"

"Just my nosy self. I live next door, remember?"

She laughed, glad there was no morning-after awkwardness. "It's just about time for you to pick up Bobby."

"I know," he said, dropping kisses on her shoulder. "What are your plans for the day?"

"Nothing special. I have an interview scheduled for Tuesday, but I already have my plane ticket. I picked up my suit from the cleaners the other day."

He straightened. "I didn't realize you were interviewing out of town."

"Sure you did. I told you."

He frowned and threw off the blanket then got out of the bed. He grabbed his jeans off the floor and stepped into them, his movements jerky. "I guess you did."

"I'm missing something here. Why are you upset?"

"Who says I'm upset? I need to get to the center, so I'll let you get dressed."

Charlotte pulled on her clothes, trying to figure out when things had gotten messed up. One minute they were laughing and the next Rick was storming out the room like a spoiled child. Morning-after awkwardness was infinitely preferable to morning-after fury.

She replayed the conversation in her mind. He'd been smiling until she mentioned the airplane ticket. Was he upset because she was sticking with her plan to leave town? Did he really think she'd throw away her plans for a new life because they'd spent one night together? A night that didn't include a word of love or promise of a future together? She'd built her life on dreams once before and had been hurt as they crashed to the ground.

Sure, she cared for him, but she wasn't going to turn her life upside down for him. Not again.

They'd had too great a time for her to leave without trying to bridge the distance between them. She heard Rick's voice and she followed it to the kitchen. He was pacing the floor, holding the telephone to his ear. The faded jeans hugging his legs and the blue shirt covering his muscular torso didn't do justice to the body she'd seen with her own eyes and caressed with her own hands. Still, he looked good enough to make her heart pound. She wanted to go into his arms, but the tension radiating from him created a barrier that stopped her where she stood. The cowardly part of her wanted to just wave and walk out, but she had too much pride to run away.

Finally he ended the call.

"What is your problem?" She jammed her hands on her hips and glared at him.

He shook his head. "A major case of the stupids. I just behaved badly."

He'd get no argument from her. "So you're not still upset with me?"

"No. Actually, I was upset with myself. But I'm over it. It's all good."

She knew he wasn't being entirely honest, but pressuring him wouldn't make him be any more forthcoming if he wasn't so inclined. And she wasn't in the mood to pacify him by promising to stick around while he tried to figure out what they were doing. "I'll leave so you can get Bobby."

He seemed to be having an internal debate. "Are you busy later?"

"I told you I didn't have any plans."

"Do you want to come over for dinner?"

"Don't you think you should ask Bobby? He might want to spend some time alone with you."

"Please. He'd choose you over me any day."

Charlotte hesitated. A day or two ago she would have said yes immediately. But last night had changed things between them. She'd known at the time that their relationship would be different, but he'd been kissing her and holding her and she hadn't cared. Now she did. The best way to deal with the confusion and awkwardness was head-on. No more trying to avoid him. That hadn't worked anyway as last night proved.

She nodded. "Okay, see you later."

Charlotte waited until the majority of the passengers had deplaned before standing. Experience had taught her that a two-hour flight turned normally civilized individuals into rude and pushy people who were determined to get off the plane before everyone else. It was as if they'd get a reward for being the first person in line at the baggage claim. She didn't understand the thrill of watching as one lone suitcase circled the carousel before all the other luggage came out.

Since she intended to fly home right after the interview, she didn't have checked baggage and didn't have to join in the march of the harried travelers. She strode through the terminal, dodging a teenager wearing a gigantic backpack who was jostling others. If she hadn't vowed to become a better person, she would have tripped him. Accidentally, of course.

Her prospective employer had arranged for a limousine to bring her to their downtown Chicago headquarters, so she looked around until she spotted a man holding a sign reading "Shields." Five minutes later she was ensconced in the back seat of the vehicle and on her way to her meeting. She pulled a portfolio from her briefcase and reviewed the information she'd gathered on the company.

Montgomery Enterprises was leading the field in advanced analytics. The executive staff was young, and from what she could tell, energetic and friendly. She'd been impressed with the people who'd conducted her telephone interview. As far as she could see, there were no negatives to being employed there. Unfortunately, she wasn't as sure about the location.

Chicago was a world-class city. She'd enjoyed several long weekends here, seeing shows, visiting museums and indulging in some major shopping along the Magnificent Mile. As with most people on vacation she hadn't paid much attention to little annoyances. Now, though, she noticed the bumper-to-bumper traffic and the aggressive driving. The number of pedestrians taking their lives into their hands as they attempted to cross the street against the light was staggering. Didn't anyone obey traffic signals?

Just then a man on a bike sped past her car window, scaring the life out of her and nearly mowing down an elderly man in the crosswalk. Before she could exhale, he'd woven his way through traffic, inciting the wrath of several motorists who laid on their horns. She didn't consider herself to be a small-town girl, but she wasn't sure she wanted to endure this headache every morning. Sure, she could get used to the commotion, but did she want to?

Deciding not to let one commute prejudice her, she focused on the positives. Chicago had a beautiful lakefront and bike paths galore. There were many dance and theater companies, so she could catch a performance at any time. And there were single men. Surely in a city of over two million she could find someone to love and who would love her in return.

What about Rick? She shut down that thought before it could take hold. Rick was in Sweet Briar, where he planned to stay. She was leaving. Although she'd begun building bridges with the people in Sweet Briar, and most of them had been receptive, the idea of a fresh start still appealed. Besides, Rick hadn't mentioned a future. She'd been swept away by her feelings years ago and had created a reality in her mind that hadn't really existed. Well, she was twelve years wiser. She wasn't going to make the same mistake twice.

The driver pulled up in front of a skyscraper on Wacker Drive, turned to her and nodded. "Have a nice day."

"Thanks." She pulled a few bills from her purse and tipped him before stepping onto the sidewalk. She pressed through the throng of people, feeling like a fish swimming against the tide until she reached the revolving doors. Finally. She stepped into an impressive lobby and glanced around. The marble floors gleamed and light streamed through the soaring windows. After checking in with security, she joined the press of humanity heading in the direction of the elevators. The company was on the twentieth floor. Naturally the elevator stopped at every floor on the way up.

A glass reception desk was visible from the elevator. Charlotte introduced herself to the smiling receptionist and was immediately shown to a comfortable seating area. A minute later a man in his early thirties came to greet her. He introduced himself as Walter Montgomery and led her to a conference room.

Five people were seated in recliners. There was no table. One man was eating a bag of chips. A woman was in her stocking feet. Everyone was dressed casually.

"We're not very formal," Walter explained. "We don't like sitting around a table being stuffy."

"Okay." That was different. She didn't consider herself stuffy, but she liked to have meetings at tables. It made taking notes easier, for one.

The interview was casual as well. There wasn't much structure. They all just sat around and talked. They complimented her on the samples of her work she'd provided and mentioned the glowing reference that Milton Hayes had provided for her. Then Walter offered her the job, mentioning a salary that nearly had her salivating. Apparently she was worth more than she knew. It was flattering, but as she toured the office meeting her potential coworkers, she knew she wouldn't accept the position. She might be changing, but this place was just a tad too relaxed for her.

On the ride back to the airport she made a list of what qualities were important to her and ranked them. Clearly money wasn't the most important factor or she would have jumped at this job; they were offering her three times what her father had paid her. Although she was willing to move to a larger city, she preferred something smaller and less congested.

The flight home was less crowded. As the plane taxied toward the gate her anticipation rose. She was looking forward to enjoying a quiet evening in her own backyard.

As she drove down her street, she saw Rick playing basketball with Bobby and her heart rate increased. Rick looked up as she pulled into her driveway and smiled. Butterflies began dancing in her stomach and she smiled back. Bobby raced to her car, pulling open her door the minute she unlocked it. He hugged her tight. Now, this was a homecoming.

"I got something for you," she said, handing him a plastic bag.

"You did?" His face lit up as he reached inside. He pulled out the gift and his mouth dropped open. "Oh, wow. A real Bulls jersey. I've wanted one my whole life."

She smiled. "That's a long time."

"It is," he agreed. Clearly he hadn't heard the irony in her voice.

Bobby yanked off his sweaty T-shirt and threw it on the driveway, then pulled on the jersey. It fit perfectly. "I look cool, don't I, Dad?"

"Totally cool."

"Wait until I show Nathaniel." Bobby hugged Charlotte again. "You are the best. I love you so much."

She kissed his head. "I love you, too."

He raced into the house, presumably to call his friend, leaving her alone with Rick.

Rick dropped a kiss onto her lips, lingering a delicious moment before he lifted his head. "Welcome home."

She leaned against his firm chest, loving the security she felt as his strong arms wrapped around her, reveling in his familiar scent. He felt like home. Of course, he wouldn't be home for long if she took a job in Chicago. There wouldn't be anyone to hug her and kiss her after a long day's work. She'd be just as alone as she was before he'd returned. "It's good to be back."

"How did it go?"

"Quite well, actually. They offered me the job."

He nodded and dropped his arms, then took a step away from her. "Wow. That's unusual. You must have knocked them off their feet."

The words were right, but there wasn't any emotion

behind them. It was as if he was the world's worst actor reading from a bad script.

"I didn't accept. I told them I needed time to decide. I have another interview scheduled for Thursday with a company in Charlotte."

"I'm sure they'll love you, too. No doubt they'll make you an offer."

Again, right words, no emotion. It was as if his support was fake. Or maybe she was reading too much into things. After all, she hadn't accepted the job, so there was nothing to celebrate.

"I imagine you're tired and want to rest. I'll see you later."

She wasn't that tired and would have liked to talk more. But he was already edging to his side of the property. "Okay. Tell Bobby I'll see him later."

He nodded and left without another word. She stared at him as he went inside his house. She thought he'd have more to say about her job and wondered why he hadn't. Deciding she was reading way too much into his actions, she went inside to shower.

Charlotte placed her order and smiled at the waitress. Wonder of wonders, the girl smiled back.

After showering, Charlotte hadn't been able to find anything she wanted to eat, so she'd decided to treat herself to a burger and fries at the diner. For half a second she considered adding a side salad but decided she hadn't changed that much.

She was grabbing a book out of her bag when a shadow fell over her table. She looked up and into the smiling face of Mayor Devlin. "Mind if I join you for a minute?"

"Not at all." Although she couldn't imagine what the

mayor would want with her, she let the book drop back into her bag.

The waitress returned with her Coke and the mayor asked for one as well. He didn't speak until they had both taken a swallow of their drinks. "I bet you're dying to know why I interrupted your dinner."

She grinned. "*Dying* might be a bit of an exaggeration, but I am curious."

"Rumor has it you no longer work for your father's company."

She swirled her straw in her drink. "That's true."

"But the grapevine hasn't discovered whether or not you've found another position."

"Slackers."

He laughed.

"No, I haven't, although I am interviewing. Why?"

"I'd like to interview you for a job with the city."

"You want to interview me?"

"Yes."

"You've lived in town long enough to know my reputation."

"Word around town is that you've been trying to make up for the past. And from what I've heard, people believe you really have changed."

"I have."

"Then I can't think of a reason why I shouldn't interview you."

"Maybe, but given your relationship with Joni, you might want to reconsider."

"What does Joni have to do with anything? She's not involved in city business."

"She's Carmen's best friend."

He raised his eyebrow, silently asking what in the world that had to do with anything.

She huffed out a breath. It wasn't airing the family's dirty laundry if most people already knew the story. "Carmen and I have been estranged for years. We're making progress, but it's slow. We've had a couple of good telephone conversations and have even met for lunch, so I'm hopeful. I want a relationship with my sister again, but the final decision is hers. Since she's Joni's friend and you're Joni's friend, you might not want to hire me."

"I never could follow complicated relationships. I still don't know the difference between a second cousin and a first cousin once removed. Are you saying we're estranged twice removed?"

She shook her head. It was obvious why he was so popular with the citizens of Sweet Briar. He had a way of putting people at ease. Not to mention he was beyond gorgeous. But she wasn't even remotely attracted to him, not with Rick around. She was getting in too deep with him, but didn't know how to stop. She'd better figure it out or else she'd end up heartbroken again.

"I don't want to cause trouble between you and Joni."

"You won't. Joni's too sweet for that. Besides, you just said that you and Carmen are no longer estranged."

"We still have a lot of ground to cover. Since I'm the one who caused the trouble, most of the walking has to be mine."

"I understand. But all that aside, would you like to hear about the position?"

Curiosity got the best of her. "Yes."

"Your degree is in marketing, correct?"

"How did you know that?"

"I have my sources." He leaned against the back of the booth and flashed her a grin. "I've seen the brochures your father's company puts out. You were listed as the executive vice president of marketing. And I have information your headhunter provided."

"Actually, I have a degree in marketing and an MBA."

He nodded. "Perfect. The job I'm looking to fill is actually a new one. Sweet Briar has become a vacation destination and we're doing quite well during the summer holidays. But we need to bring in tourists year-round as well as attract other businesses. If this position is something that might interest you, we can set up a meeting and talk in more detail."

"Actually, it sounds intriguing." She paused. "I'm interested."

"Good." He grabbed a business card from his pocket and handed it to her. Then he lifted his cup and drained it, not bothering with a straw. "Call my office and set up an appointment at your convenience. The earlier the better."

"Will do." The mayor's offer went against her plan to leave yet she was actually considering it. Her determination to leave Sweet Briar wasn't as strong as before. People had been forgiving and welcoming. And then there were Rick and Bobby, who were becoming the two most important people in her life. If she got this job, she wouldn't have to leave them. Things were looking positive between her and Rick. They might actually have a future if she was willing to take a chance on him.

Chapter Eighteen

Rick sat on his patio and stared at the night sky. The wind was blowing hard, whipping the leaves on the trees and blowing petals off Charlotte's flowers and spraying them over his lawn. The scent of rain filled the air. Dark clouds were moving in rapidly. No doubt fat drops would be raining down from the sky in the next ten minutes or so. Lightning flashed in the distance, turning the sky an eerie yellow. The weather was definitely in tune with his mood.

Charlotte was leaving Sweet Briar. Maybe not tomorrow or the next day, but soon. And probably forever. Given the state of her relationship with her family—or lack thereof—there was nothing holding her here. He'd hoped their growing relationship would be reason enough for her to consider remaining. Apparently not.

He could deal with it. It would be painful to lose her, but he was a grown man and knew things didn't always work out. And he'd left her twelve years ago to pursue his dreams, so it was only fair that he let her do the same now without pressure from him. And when he thought about it, he'd completed his mission. He'd come back to Sweet Briar to make amends to Charlotte and had done so. Maybe letting her go to live her life happily somewhere else was the fulfillment of his goal.

But what about Bobby? Bobby was a child. He'd already suffered more than his share of loss. He was finally over being left behind by Sherry and was becoming the happy child he used to be.

Rick slammed his hand on the table, venting the anger surging through him. His son was going to be hurt when Charlotte moved away and Rick was to blame. He'd known Charlotte had been considering leaving town, yet he'd encouraged the relationship between Bobby and Charlotte. She'd reached Bobby in ways Rick hadn't been able to do. Bobby loved Charlotte. He was going to be devastated when she left.

The wind blew and rain splattered onto his face and chest. Rick jumped to his feet just as the clouds burst. Water came down in sheets. By the time he'd raced up the steps and into the kitchen, he was drenched. He yanked off his wet shirt and swiped at the moisture as he climbed the stairs. He flipped the wall switch to turn on the overhead light in his bedroom. Nothing.

Lightning flashed, momentarily illuminating the dark room. Booming thunder followed, rattling the windows.

"Dad!" Bobby yelled as he ran into the room.

"It's okay, son." He gave Bobby a quick hug. "It's just a little storm."

"I'm not scared," Bobby replied as he trailed Rick across the room. When Rick stopped at his dresser, his son bumped into him.

"You sure you're not scared? It's all right if you are."

"No. I'm concerned."

Rick smiled, grateful for the darkness that covered his expression. "You can sleep with me if you want."

A flash of lightning lit the room as Bobby dashed to Rick's bed. Hopping in, he burrowed under the thin blanket. Rick swapped his jeans for pajama bottoms and resigned himself to getting kicked most of the night.

"I was just thinking."

"About what?" Rick asked, sitting on the edge of the bed.

"Charlotte. She's all alone and probably scared. We should call her and make sure she's okay."

Of course Bobby's first thought would be of Charlotte. He adored her. "It's nearly midnight. She's probably sleeping."

Thunder rolled again, this time longer and more loudly. The entire house shook.

"We should call her," Bobby insisted. "She's probably awake just like we are."

Rick recognized the stubbornness in his son's voice. Neither of them was going to get any sleep until Bobby was assured Charlotte was safe. Since Rick had patients to treat in the morning, he couldn't debate all night. He really needed to prepare Bobby for the time when Charlotte was no longer a part of their lives. But not tonight when Rick was having a hard enough time preparing himself.

Grabbing the landline, Rick pressed the first button. He'd put her number in speed dial in case Bobby needed to reach her. He needn't have bothered. Bobby had committed her number to memory.

Charlotte answered on the first ring.

"It's Rick."

"And Bobby," his son chimed in, digging his chin into Rick's shoulder. "Tell her I'm here, too."

"And Bobby," he repeated. "We're checking to make sure you're all right."

"See if she wants to come over and sleep with us. She's probably scared all by herself."

Charlotte laughed. "I heard that. Let Bobby know I appreciate the offer but I'm fine."

Rick relayed her message to his son, who yawned and closed his eyes. "I didn't want to bother you but Bobby insisted."

"That's all right. The storm woke me up before you did."

Her voice was slightly husky with sleep and he remembered how perfect it felt to hold her as she slept. She'd been so sweet. So warm. He'd give anything to have her in his arms right now. Since that was impossible, he needed to end the conversation before he did something stupid like beg her not to leave him. She wanted a fresh start away from Sweet Briar. He needed to respect her wish. "I'll say good-night so you can get back to sleep."

He heard her sharp intake of breath and knew his tone had been harsher than he'd intended. He hoped he hadn't hurt her feelings. "Good night."

The phone clicked as she hung up. Man, doing the right thing sucked.

Charlotte smiled as she exited the office building and walked down the busy Charlotte street. The sunny day suited her mood. The interview had gone great. She liked the people she'd be working with. The position would be challenging enough to keep her on her toes with a salary commensurate with her experience and responsibilities. The city was the right size, with plenty of cultural activities to fill her spare time. And it was only two hours away from Sweet Briar. So why had she told them she needed time before making a decision?

Sure, it was never a good idea to accept a job offer on the spot, but it was more than conventional wisdom that had her hesitating. Her relationship with Rick had her questioning her decision to leave Sweet Briar. Did they have a future? No matter how often she told herself to remember how badly she'd been hurt by him, she couldn't help hoping things would work out between them this time. But even though her feelings for Rick had grown, she didn't think he felt the same.

He had begun pulling back from her. When Bobby stopped by every evening, Rick made excuses to avoid joining them. Not only that, he'd started coming to get Bobby twenty minutes after he'd arrived, barely giving his son enough time to eat his snack and share the events of his day.

If she didn't know better she would think he was ending things. She remembered how she had begged him not to end their engagement and how he'd left her behind, not giving her a thought for twelve years.

She certainly wasn't going to plead like that again. One humiliation was more than a lifetime's worth. If he wanted to walk out of their relationship, she wasn't going to grab his ankles and hold on to him. It would hurt like heck to let him go because she'd once again stupidly fallen in love with him, but she would take that secret to the grave. She might be trying to become a better person, but she still had her pride.

The hard part would be maintaining her relationship with Bobby. Rick might be trying to ease her out of his son's life, but she wasn't going. Bobby had suffered enough when his mother walked out on him. There was no way Charlotte would do the same. Rick should be smart enough to know that, but if he wasn't, she'd tell him. She loved Bobby and she wasn't going to hurt him. She and Rick needed to get along for Bobby's sake. Once she was settled, she'd invite him to spend a weekend with her. Maybe they could take in a Hornets game. And she'd come back to Sweet Briar on a regular basis to visit him.

She spent the entire ride back from Charlotte mulling things over. By the time she pulled onto her street, she was both relieved to be home and apprehensive about encountering Rick. She immediately saw him on his front stoop, watching Bobby dribble the basketball in the driveway.

"How was your interview?" Bobby asked as soon as she got out of the car. He had become her biggest cheerleader, a stark contrast to his father, who'd grown increasingly negative by the day. Rick walked up behind Bobby slowly, and she wondered if he was listening.

"It was great. They offered me the job." She lifted her chin as she answered. She wasn't going to let Rick's negativity bring her down.

"It's funny that your name is Charlotte and you might move to a city named Charlotte."

She smiled. "Yes, it is."

"I wonder if there's a city named Bobby. Or Robert since that's my real name. Do you think there is one?"

"I wouldn't be surprised. We can always look on the internet. Have you had dinner yet?"

He nodded. "Yeah, but I didn't have dessert. Just an apple. Dad thinks an apple is dessert. I don't."

"Neither do I. Lucky for you I have cookies and ice cream. You can put cookies in your ice cream if you want."

"Great."

Rick placed his hands on his son's shoulders, halting him before he could dash up the stairs. "Charlotte had a long drive home. She's probably tired. You can have ice cream some other time."

Lips compressed, she spun and faced Rick. "I'm not tired. And even if I was, Bobby would still be welcome."

She turned on her heels and stalked up the stairs before Rick could see the pain in her eyes. How could he try to yank Bobby from her life? Did he think she didn't have feelings? She did, and he was stomping all over them. She knew he was probably trying to protect Bobby from getting hurt, but that didn't make her feel better. It irritated her that he didn't give her credit for caring about Bobby's feelings. She didn't want Bobby to be hurt, either.

Charlotte unlocked her door, letting Bobby inside. He turned and peered around her. "Aren't you coming, Dad?"

Rick hesitated as if searching for an excuse. Apparently he couldn't find one. "Sure. I could use some dessert myself."

Charlotte managed to cover her surprise. Now he wanted to be around her? The man was nothing if not confusing. "You guys go ahead and get started. I'm going to get out of this suit. I'll be down in a minute."

And hopefully when she returned she would have a better understanding of just what was going on in Rick's head.

What in the world was he thinking? He was supposed to be easing Charlotte from their lives. Instead, he was sitting on her back patio, polishing off a big bowl of Oreo cookies and vanilla ice cream and trying not to stare at her mouth. Every time she spooned some of the treat between her lips, she gave a sexy little moan that was dangerously arousing. Given that his son was sitting across the table, indulging in his own dessert, Rick's reaction was totally inappropriate. Worse, when the three of them were together like this, he could envision their lives together. Was he making a mistake by not pressing Charlotte to stay in Sweet Briar and give their relationship a chance?

He managed to stop staring at her lips and look into her eyes. "So…you have a big decision to make. Chicago or Charlotte."

"Not really. I already decided that Chicago is out of the running."

"Really?"

"It wasn't a good fit. The people were nice but the company was too laid-back for me. I don't want a place as staid as my father's company, but something in the middle would suit me just fine."

"Too bad. We could have gone to some Bulls games," Bobby interjected before scooping more ice cream into his messy mouth. "I always wanted to do that."

"That would have been great," she agreed.

"What did you think about the company in Charlotte?" Rick hadn't meant to ask, but suddenly he needed to know.

"They seemed like people I could work with. And the job sounded interesting. I could be happy there."

In Charlotte. Away from him. Charlotte was much closer to Sweet Briar than Chicago, but it was still a couple of hours away. He couldn't imagine that she'd want to drive that distance every day. It wouldn't be conducive to having any type of life. She might try for a while, but eventually she would end up relocating.

She and Bobby had their heads together, whispering about something. Bobby glanced over at him then quickly away when he realized Rick was watching. Rick tried not to feel left out, but wasn't entirely successful.

"Hey, Dad," Bobby said, dropping his spoon into his empty bowl. "I was wondering if I could sleep over here tonight."

"Why?"

"Because."

He shook his head. Didn't Charlotte see what she was doing? Didn't she care? Bobby loved her and was growing more attached every day. Surely she knew how destroyed Bobby would be when she left. He knew how badly he himself would hurt watching Charlotte drive away for the last time. "Not tonight. In fact, you should say good-night now and head on home."

"What about you?"

"I want to talk to Charlotte for a few minutes."

Bobby looked like he wanted to argue, but then he suddenly smiled. No doubt the poor kid thought this was part of Rick's plan to make Charlotte fall in love with him. He didn't have the heart to tell him there was no way that was going to happen. Not with Charlotte leaving them behind. She had a right to be happy and free from the past. If moving away from Sweet Briar was what it took, then it was only fair that he let her go. Still, she should have considered Bobby's feelings. She should be helping Rick ease Bobby from her life, not pulling him in closer.

"Sure." Bobby gave Charlotte a hug then looked back at him. "Is it okay if I practice free throws until you come home?"

"Yes."

Bobby flashed a thumbs-up sign before he disappeared into Charlotte's house. A few seconds later, Rick heard the front door slam followed by the dribble of a basketball.

Rick told himself to stay calm but couldn't. "Just what game are you playing?" he said without preamble.

Her eyes narrowed and he couldn't help noticing just how cute she looked despite being angry. "Excuse me?"

"Why did you invite Bobby to spend the night with you?"

"I didn't. I told him I bought a new DVD and he asked if he could stay over and watch it with me."

"Oh."

She stood and slammed her hands onto her slim hips. "Yeah, oh."

Feeling he was losing control of the conversation, he stood, too, hoping his greater height would shift the balance of power into his favor. "I just don't understand what's going on here."

"I'm not playing games, that's for sure, and I resent you accusing me of that."

"I'm concerned about Bobby. I don't want him to be hurt when you leave."

She nodded slowly. The indignation in her eyes turned to deep sadness. "I get it. You just assume that I'm going to hurt him."

His stomach churned at her sorrow. He hadn't meant to hurt her. "Not purposely. I know you love him, but he's bound to be hurt when you leave him behind."

"So you're going to keep us apart. That's your plan, right?"

"Yes."

"It's a stupid plan."

"Maybe, but Bobby's my son, so I make all the decisions concerning his welfare."

"Fine." She clamped her lips closed as if she were holding back words. Her chest heaved with angry breaths. "You can leave now. And don't come back. I don't want to hurt you, either. I know how that feels."

His insides froze at her parting shot and his fury burned hotter. "I didn't think this was some type of payback. At least not before. Was this part of some sick plan? Were you trying to get me to fall in love with you so I would know how it felt to be left behind?"

"Are you saying you're in love with me?" The mocking tone in her voice was painful. Apparently she wasn't in love with him.

He wouldn't give her the satisfaction of knowing how much he'd come to care for her. "That's not what I said. But nice dodge. I notice you didn't answer my question. But tell me, Charlotte, was your need for revenge so great you would hurt an already hurting child?"

"Right. My need to work has nothing to do with anything. It's all about you. I've spent the past twelve years plotting my revenge. You figured it out." She shook her head. "Your ego is so big I'm surprised you can carry it around."

"Charlotte…" His voice trailed off as he realized how stupid he'd been. He knew she wasn't heartless or vengeful. And she certainly would never hurt Bobby.

"Just go. And don't come back."

Chapter Nineteen

Charlotte dressed with care for her interview with the mayor. Too bad things had ended the way they had with Rick, because this job sounded like something she'd enjoy. And under other circumstances, if it was offered to her, she would accept it. But she'd foolishly fallen in love with Rick and he'd told her point-blank he didn't love her. The past was repeating itself. Her heart would never heal if she lived in the same town with him, hoping he'd one day return her feelings. So she was accepting the other job and moving. Grabbing her purse, she left her house and climbed into her car.

The ride to city hall was short. For the first time in a long while, she actually looked at the scenery. The trees were filled with large green leaves that swayed in the gentle breeze. Flowerpots bursting with colorful blooms were strategically placed along the sidewalk. There were numerous black iron benches on either side of the road, where vacationers were taking a break from shopping and locals were sitting and visiting with friends.

The benches were new. Mayor Devlin had begun making little improvements since the beginning of his tenure. Many of the old guard had fought him tooth and nail about the expenditure, but he'd been up to the challenge. He'd won the battle and Sweet Briar was better for it. He'd been reelected last fall in a landslide.

Charlotte parked on the street and headed into city hall. The building looked the same as it had all her life. Her respect for the mayor grew as she realized he'd spent taxpayer dollars on improvements that would benefit the citizens and not wasted it on cosmetic changes that would benefit only himself.

Denise Harper, the longtime secretary for many mayors, looked up as Charlotte entered. She smiled professionally and led the way to the mayor's office.

"Good morning," he said, rising and circling his sleek, uncluttered desk. He offered his hand. "You're right on time."

"Good morning," she replied, shaking his hand.

He led her to a seating group in the corner, waiting until she took a spot on the sofa before sitting in a chair across from her. She felt so comfortable with him. She would have liked working for him. Too bad she had to leave town. "I've taken a good look at the packet your human resources recruiter provided. It's quite impressive."

"Thanks. I enjoyed the work. It was often challenging, but always fulfilling."

He nodded. "Let me tell you a bit about the position. It's a new one, so you'll have a lot of freedom to make it what it needs to be. Within reason, of course," he added with a grin. "That's the good news. The bad news is the salary." He mentioned a number that was lower than what she'd been making, but not insultingly so.

"I can live with that."

He nodded. "You've lived in Sweet Briar all of your life, so you're well aware of what we have and what we lack. Your job would be to work with me to keep improving the town and publicizing those improvements. Right now we have several businesses geared specifically for tourists and a few small businesses that serve the town. We need more. Don't worry. I'm not trying to turn Sweet Briar into another Chicago or New York."

"Thank goodness," Charlotte replied.

"But we can grow and offer more amenities without losing what makes us special. For instance, I've been looking into the possibility of attracting a minor-league baseball team. I'm also considering the feasibility of building a theater where we could produce shows throughout the year."

"You could attract traveling shows and concerts," she mused. "You would need an in-house director. And a fund-raiser. Not to mention a group of actors and staff to put on productions to fill out the year."

"True. But if we do things right, we can draw visitors from neighboring states."

She leaned forward, her interest growing. "What else are you thinking about?"

He smiled as if he knew he had hooked her. For the next twenty minutes he outlined plans for projects. Not all of them could be undertaken immediately. Some wouldn't happen for another five or seven years. But they would help Sweet Briar to prosper without compromising the essence of the town. She tossed out a couple of suggestions of her own, thinking of ways to improve his plans.

Finally he leaned back in his chair. "What do you think?"

"I think you're brilliant."

"Well, that goes without saying. But feel free to say it to whoever you can get to listen. I meant about the job. Do you want it?"

"I do." The words were out of her mouth before she could stop them. They were a truth from her very soul. This job would be a perfect fit for her. "But I can't take it."

"Why not? Is it money? I might be able to find a couple thousand more dollars, but not much more."

"No. I would love if the salary was higher, but no one works for small-town government in order to get rich."

"That's true. So what is the problem? If it's something I can fix, I will." He asked the question as if he was her friend and not her potential boss.

To her horror, her eyes filled with tears. She hated crying, especially in front of people. And during a job interview, no less. She blinked rapidly, hoping he wouldn't notice. "I have to leave town."

"Why?"

"Because."

He raised an eyebrow but didn't say anything. She could get up and leave with her pride intact, but didn't. Despite not knowing him well, she could tell he wanted to help. Before she knew what was happening, the words were tumbling out of her mouth.

"It's Rick."

"Tyler?"

"Yes. We were dating, but now it's over."

"I'm sorry."

"I can't stay in Sweet Briar. Seeing him would hurt too much."

"I understand." Mayor Devlin drummed his fingers against his thigh. "I'll tell you what. I know you'll be perfect for the job, so I'll keep the position open for a few weeks, just in case things work out between you and Rick."

"I don't see how they can. Thanks for the positive thought, though."

"On the chance that you decide to take the job, let's talk a bit more about the duties."

Charlotte nodded, pleased to stop talking about Rick Tyler and her broken heart.

Rick sat at the kitchen table, dreading the conversation he was about to have with his son. Two days had passed since Charlotte had kicked him out of her life and told him to never come back. He might have had a chance to make up for being an idiot if she wasn't leaving town. But she'd taken a job in a city two hours away. He hadn't wanted to face the facts before, but now he needed to. Charlotte was leaving.

Rick hoped Bobby wouldn't be crushed the way he'd been when Sherry left him behind. The way Rick felt now.

"Hey, Dad," Bobby said as he grabbed a bowl and filled it with cereal. Several flakes landed on the table but as usual he didn't seem to notice. Most of the milk actually made it into the bowl, though, which was an improvement. Generally at least a quarter of it splashed over the rim.

"Hey." He rubbed a hand over his face. "I want to talk to you."

Bobby lifted his spoon to his mouth. "About what?"

Rick's chest ached as he forced out the words. "Charlotte is moving."

"I know," Bobby said before he shoveled in the cereal. "She has a new job."

"Right. And Charlotte is a couple hours away from here."

"Charlotte the city is. Our Charlotte is next door." Bobby laughed. "I still think it's funny that the city has her name."

"Yes, well, she'll have to move. Charlotte is leaving us and there is nothing we can do."

Bobby set his spoon beside his half-eaten bowl of cereal. "That's not true. She loves me."

Rick couldn't let his son doubt that he was loved. "Don't worry, Bobby. I will never leave you. I'm here for the long haul."

"Charlotte loves me," Bobby repeated, though his voice wobbled. "She told me."

"Of course she does," Rick replied.

"Then ask her to marry you."

"She won't. Even though she loves you, she doesn't love me," Rick admitted, the painful words slicing his heart.

Bobby's eyes filled with tears that began running down his cheeks. "You were supposed to make her fall in love with you but you didn't. You never even tried. You didn't have a plan and got waylaid."

Despite the situation, he smiled at Bobby's word choice. "Yes, I did."

"No, you didn't." Bobby slammed his fist against the table. He stood so fast he knocked over his chair. "I did my part. She knows I think she's special. She loves me. You didn't do anything."

"I gave her some chocolate and flowers," Rick said lamely, although why he was defending himself to his son was beyond his comprehension. Perhaps because he wanted to justify himself. Maybe he was trying to convince himself that he'd done all he could. That he hadn't let his fear of being hurt hold him back.

"That's it? She has flowers in her yard. And anybody can go to the store and get candy. You gave her what she already had." Bobby was glaring through his tears.

"It doesn't have anything to do with candy."

"Then think of something else."

"There is nothing else."

"Well, then I'm sorry for you." Bobby dragged his arm across his face, drying his tears. "But I'm not staying here. I'm going with Charlotte."

He had to have heard that wrong. "What?"

"I'm going with Charlotte. I'll miss Nathaniel because he's my best friend, but I'll come back and visit him. If you'll get me a phone I can call him or text him sometimes."

Rick's head was spinning. Did Bobby think he could just switch out one parent for another? Of course he did. Why wouldn't he? That was exactly what Sherry had done. When she didn't want to be a mother any longer she'd found him a dad. Now Bobby was trading him in for a new mother. That hurt, but Rick needed to stay calm, so he mirrored his son's words. "You're going to move."

"You can come, too."

"I have to stay here. I'm the town's doctor, remember?" He'd committed to stay for two years. Although he hadn't signed a contract, he'd given his word. His reputation would be shot if he closed his practice after only a couple of months. And what about the people of Sweet Briar? He didn't want to be one more doctor who'd let them down.

Bobby rolled his eyes. "Of course I remember. You're my dad."

Relief flooded Rick at those words. Maybe Bobby was starting to see reason. He was calmer now at least.

"But you can work anywhere. Everybody needs doctors. But Charlotte can't live here if her job is somewhere else. So we have to go with her."

"It's not that easy. Sweet Briar is our home and this is where we're staying. Charlotte may be moving, but we aren't going with her."

"Why not? Don't you love her?"

Sure he loved her. That was never a question. But what difference did it make now? He'd hurt Charlotte and she was through with him. She'd forgiven him for the past but his lack of faith in her and his baseless accusation had been the last straw. He didn't see a way to come back from that.

He paused. Was he really willing to let her walk out of his life without a fight? Was his acceptance an excuse for not having to change his life? He loved her but what had he been willing to give up for her? Not too much. Shame filled him as he realized he'd expected Charlotte to sacrifice her dreams for him. True, he believed she could be happy in Sweet Briar—she and Carmen were making progress in their relationship and Charlotte was making friends   but she didn't.

He looked into his son's face and decided giving up wasn't an option. He was going to fight for what he wanted. It was time to show her how much he loved her and that meant being where she needed him to be. He was going to win Charlotte back.

Charlotte tossed the folded bath towel into a box and tried to ignore the pain in her heart. She had too much packing to do for her to waste time throwing herself a pity party. She'd played the game and lost. There was nothing more to do. She certainly wasn't going to complain about the deck being stacked against her. You could only play the cards you'd been dealt.

She took a shallow breath. How long would it take until she was able to breathe without her chest hurting? *Please, not as long as last time.*

The doorbell rang long and loud, a clear signal that Bobby was here. She hurried to the door. He was such a wonderful boy. How could her heart survive not seeing him every day? She loved him like a son. If she lived to be a hundred she would never understand his mother's decision to leave him behind. Leaving was tearing her heart out but she had no intention of cutting him out of her life. She and Rick might not have made it as a couple, but surely they could be adult enough about the breakup to do what was right for Bobby.

"Hi, Charlotte," he said the minute she opened the door. "What are you doing?"

She grinned at the sight of him. "Packing. What are you doing?"

"Taking a break from packing."

"Where are you going?" He hadn't mentioned a field trip.

"With you."

She sank onto the sofa and pulled him down beside her. She thought her heart had already splintered into as many pieces as possible. She'd been wrong. "Oh, Bobby. I would love to take you with me, but I can't. Your dad would miss you too much."

"No, he won't."

"I know you were angry at your father when you first arrived, but you know he loves you very much."

"I know that now."

"Then you know your place is with him. You can't leave him."

"He can come, too, if he wants. But I'm coming with you."

Charlotte closed her eyes on a wave of guilt. Bobby truly believed he was coming with her. He was even packing. Rick had warned her that Bobby was getting too attached, and she'd gotten angry. He'd been right. Now she had to do her best to fix things and protect Bobby's heart. "I need to talk to your dad."

He shrugged. "Okay."

They walked out her door and started across the lawn. He stopped and picked up his basketball. "I think I'll stay out here and let you guys talk."

Charlotte hesitated before ringing the doorbell. Although she didn't want to see Rick, she had to let him know what Bobby hoped. If he'd let her, she'd help him deal with Bobby's feelings. Maybe he'd be willing to let his son visit her from time to time. She tried to order her thoughts, but as the door swung open, she realized it had been an exercise in futility. Her brain didn't function properly around Rick.

"Charlotte." His eyebrows rose as he stared at her and she readied herself for another battle. Then he smiled and relief made her legs go weak. "What are you doing here?"

"I need to talk to you."

"Sure." He let her inside then led her to the sofa.

She blew out a breath and got straight to it. "Bobby told me he was moving with me."

"You've seen Bobby?"

She noticed that he didn't address her comment. Maybe he didn't think it was a big deal. "Yes. He came over a few minutes ago. He said he was taking a break from packing."

"A break? We just started." He shook his head. "He just wanted to see you."

"What do you mean? Why are you packing?"

"Because we're moving."

"You're moving?"

"Yes."

Her heart thumped, and hope grew. "To where?"

He shook his head. "I'm so sorry."

Her heart dropped and her hope died a painful death. They weren't moving to be with her. Had she really thought they would? Perhaps now that he and Bobby had a good relationship, they were moving back to Milwaukee. She stood. "You don't need to apologize. I never seriously thought we had a future."

"You didn't?"

She turned her head and looked away, willing the tears in her eyes to dry up. Instead, one slid down her cheek. "No."

He brushed it away with his thumb. "I'm sorry. I didn't mean to hurt you again, but I did."

"It's okay."

"No, it's not." He cupped her face and looked into her eyes. The love she saw there took her breath away. "We're coming with you."

"You're coming with me?" She sputtered. "What about your practice?"

"I'm going to try to find someone to take over."

"But the people in Sweet Briar need a doctor now. Nathaniel's mom is sick. Carmen's going to have twins."

"I know. But you come first. You always should have. I left you before. I'm not making that mistake again. We belong together. So if you go, we go."

Tears overflowed her eyes and ran down her cheeks. But these were happy tears. She'd always wanted him to love her. To want to be with her. He'd run from her in the past, breaking her heart. But now he was actually following her, willing to give up everything to be with her. He was choosing to be with her. He was putting her first. She shook her head. "You don't need to do that, Rick. I'll stay in Sweet Briar."

"No. You want a fresh start somewhere nobody knows you. You have a new job."

"I'm not going to take it. Mayor Devlin offered me a job I really would like."

"When?"

"The other day."

"Hmm. That's interesting. When I told him that I was moving, he didn't get upset or try to talk me out of it. He just smiled."

Charlotte's cheeks grew warm. "I might have told him a little bit about us."

"You might have, huh?" Rick grinned and pulled her close. His familiar yet sexy scent surrounded her.

"Definitely."

"I might have mentioned you, too."

She rested her head on his strong shoulder. "So what arc wc going to do?"

"The choice is yours. Think about it and decide."

She didn't hesitate. "I want to stay. I'll call the human resources manager in Charlotte and let him know I can't take the job. Then I'll call Mayor Devlin. And you can keep your practice going here."

"Are you sure?"

"Yes. Bobby's happy here. We can't uproot him."

"He'd go to the ends of the earth if you were there.

He threatened to leave me behind if I didn't get with the program."

"Really?"

"Yes. I was so worried he would feel abandoned when you left. But still I didn't even consider going with you. I was afraid you wouldn't want me. That you were getting even with me for leaving you before. Bobby made me realize possibilities I hadn't even considered."

"Hey. What's going on?" Bobby asked, coming into the room. She hadn't noticed when the dribbling stopped.

"Charlotte and I were talking."

"Did you tell her we're going with her?"

"Yes. But we decided not to move."

"What do you mean?" Bobby's eyes narrowed and his voice rose. "You said we could go with Charlotte."

Charlotte reached out and snagged Bobby's hand. "He means that we're all staying in Sweet Briar."

"But what about your job? You have bills to pay and need money."

"I'm taking a job working for the mayor."

He smiled broadly. "Good. I'm going to tell Nathaniel we're staying here. Are you going to marry Dad and become my stepmother?"

"Your father hasn't asked me yet."

Bobby slapped a hand across his forehead and stared at his dad. "I'm going to come up with a plan. If we wait for you, you and Charlotte will never get married."

"Not this time. I know what to do. You just go call Nathaniel."

"Okay." Bobby took a step and then stopped and turned around and looked at her. "Just in case Dad doesn't get it right, I'll tell you. He loves you and wants to marry you. Okay?"

Charlotte nodded and managed to suppress a giggle. He was just so serious.

"Go." Rick swatted at his son, who galloped out of the room and up the stairs, making typical boy noise.

"Do you have a plan?" Charlotte asked, grinning.

"Yes." He hopped off the couch and raced up the stairs, making slightly less noise than his son. A minute later he was back, a boyish grin on his face.

"You get last-minute instructions from Bobby?"

He shook his head at her teasing, then crossed the room, coming to stand in front of her. He knelt and took her hand into his. "I love you, Charlotte. So much. Will you marry me and make me the happiest man in the world? I promise to never leave. I'll do everything in my power to make you happy."

"I love you, too. And yes, I'll marry you."

He reached into his pocket and pulled out a diamond ring. Smiling, he slipped it onto her finger, then brushed his lips over her knuckles. "I'll make you happy."

She sighed. "I already am."

Before either of them could speak, Bobby came thundering down the stairs. "Did you ask her yet?"

"He did. And I said yes."

"Good. So can you get married tomorrow? That way you can start being my stepmom right away."

Rick clapped a hand on his son's shoulder. "I hate to tell you this, but women like weddings and dresses. They need time to plan."

Bobby rolled his eyes. "I hope you're better at planning than Dad."

Charlotte laughed and hugged him. "I am. I promise we'll get married soon."

Rick put his arm around them both. "I'm counting on that."

Charlotte smiled. Their second chance at love was even sweeter than the first. And she was getting a second chance in Sweet Briar. A month ago she wouldn't have believed it was possible, but she finally had everything she ever wanted.

* * * * *

*If you enjoyed Charlotte and Rick's story,
don't miss the next installment
of Kathy Douglass's
Sweet Briar Sweethearts series,*
The Rancher's Return,
*coming March 2019
from Harlequin Special Edition.*

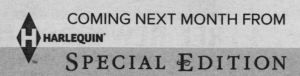

#1 *New York Times* bestselling author

LINDA LAEL MILLER

presents:

The next great contemporary read from Harlequin Special Edition author Brenda Harlen! A touching story about the magic of creating a family and developing romantic relationships.

The cutest threesome in Haven is still in diapers.

Opening Haven's first boutique hotel is Liam Gilmore's longtime dream come true, especially when he hires alluring Macy Clayton as manager. Good thing the single mother's already spoken for—by her adorable eight-month-old triplets! Because Liam isn't looking for forever after. Then why is the playboy rancher fantasizing about a future with Macy and her trio of tiny charmers?

Available January 15, wherever books are sold.

"You kissed me," he reminded her.

"The first time," she acknowledged.

"You kissed me back the second time."

"Has any woman ever not kissed you back?" she
wondered.

"I'm not interested in any other woman right now," he
told her. "I'm only interested in you."

The intensity of his gaze made her belly flutter. "I've
got three kids," she reminded him.

"That's not what's been holding me back."

"What's holding you back?"

"I'm trying to respect our working relationship."

"Yeah, that complicates things," she agreed. Then she finished the wine in her glass and pushed away from the table. "Will you excuse me for a minute? I just want to give my mom a call to check on the kids."

"Of course," he agreed. "But I can't promise the rest of that tart will be there when you get back."

She gave one last, lingering glance at the pastry before she said, "You can finish the tart."

He was tempted by the dessert, but he managed to resist. He didn't know how much longer he could hold out against his attraction to Macy—or if she wanted him to.

Had he crossed a line by flirting with her? She hadn't reacted in a way that suggested she was upset or offended, but she hadn't exactly flirted back, either.

"Is everything okay?" he asked when she returned to the table several minutes later.

She nodded. "I got caught in the middle of an argument."

"With your mom?"

"With myself."

His brows lifted. "Did you win?"

"I hope so," she said.

Then she set an antique key on the table and slid it toward him.

Don't miss
Claiming the Cowboy's Heart *by Brenda Harlen,*
available February 2019 wherever
Harlequin® Special Edition *books and ebooks are sold.*

www.Harlequin.com

Looking for more satisfying love stories
with community and family at their core?

Check out **Harlequin® Special Edition**
and **Love Inspired®** books!

New books available every month!

CONNECT WITH US AT:

Facebook.com/groups/HarlequinConnection

Facebook.com/HarlequinBooks

Twitter.com/HarlequinBooks

Instagram.com/HarlequinBooks

Pinterest.com/HarlequinBooks

ReaderService.com

H HARLEQUIN®

**ROMANCE WHEN
YOU NEED IT**

HFGENRE2018

Love Harlequin romance?

DISCOVER.

Be the first to find out about promotions, news and exclusive content!

Facebook.com/HarlequinBooks

Twitter.com/HarlequinBooks

Instagram.com/HarlequinBooks

Pinterest.com/HarlequinBooks

ReaderService.com

EXPLORE.

Sign up for the Harlequin e-newsletter and download a free book from any series at **TryHarlequin.com.**

CONNECT.

Join our Harlequin community to share your thoughts and connect with other romance readers!
Facebook.com/groups/HarlequinConnection

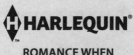

HARLEQUIN®

**ROMANCE WHEN
YOU NEED IT**